Running from the Flames

Sonia Hale

Copyright © 2024 by Sonia Hale

All rights reserved.

No portion of this book may be reproduced in any form without written permission from the publisher or author, except as permitted by U.S. copyright law.

Contents

1. Chapter 1 — 1
2. Chapter 2 — 10
3. Chapter 3 — 19
4. Chapter 4 — 25
5. Chapter 5 — 30
6. Chapter 6 — 36
7. Chapter 7 — 42
8. Chapter 8 — 46
9. Chapter 9 — 52
10. Chapter 10 — 56
11. Chapter 11 — 61
12. Chapter 12 — 67
13. Chapter 13 — 73
14. Chapter 14 — 80

15.	Chapter 15	85
16.	Chapter 16	92
17.	Chapter 17	98
18.	Chapter 18	104
19.	Chapter 19	115
20.	Epilogue	130

Chapter 1

Hello I am Brey Z. Rena, I am sixteen and here is my life. I attended Northside high school in Roanoke Virginia. Today is Friday, so it will be like every other Friday for the past seven years. I'll wake up at seven, shower, get dressed, eat breakfast, go to school for four hours, then go to track, target practice, fencing, boxing, knife throwing, karate, and finally home. At home my mom and I make dinner, and we eat as a family.

At the head of the table sat my father Lewis Rena. My dad loved jokes, pranks, and just getting in to trouble, he is laid back, and enjoyed building things. He is five ten with a large build, chocolate skin, dark brown eyes, and jet black hair. Like all fathers, he is very protective of my sisters and me, but behind that facade he is a big teddy bear. My mother sat to my left, Kita Rena, a sweet, loving, and kind person. If there was anything wrong she is who I would go to. She is five four with mocha skin, hazelnut eyes and dark brown hair. She loved cooking and I loved cooking with her.

Across from me sat my little sister, Jackie Rena, a snappy, short tempered, fashionista. Her life goal is to be a fashion designer, and she is the president of the fashion marketing club. She is a complete social butterfly and squirms in silence. Like my mom, she has mocha skin, dark brown eyes, and dark brown hair. To the right of her sat her twin, Jazz Rena, a headstrong, competitive, opinionated, short tempered, and Like every other fourteen-year-old she feels misunderstood. She could have been a carbon copy of my mom, but two inches taller. Unlike her twin, she took an interest in sports, track and archery to be pacific.

While at dinner my parents were extremely quiet, and when I asked them what was wrong they gave each other a weird look then said it was something with work. My parents almost never spoke about work except that they work for a private company in the justice system.

I just assumed that whatever it was it would be complicated and after dinner went to sleep. When I woke up the next morning I was ecstatic because every Saturday we would all go to the movies and the movie to my favorite book had just came out, best friends and the cute guy, It's this movie where two girls have to save the guy they love from the mafia. It was Jackie's turn to pick, and she chose this animated spy movie.

I felt like I lost a piece of my life in that theater Jackie left us and sat in the back with her friends. When we finally left the theater and we were stuck in traffic, and after an hour we turned down a side street then came to an intersection then a set of headlights came hurdling towards us.

I saw my life in flashes leave our apartment in Richmond traveling to London, Tokyo, Moscow, Rio, Paris, Mumbai, Mexico City, every week a new city, country, or even continent. By the time I was eight I spoke four languages and experienced hotels around the world. Then my parents bought a house in Blacksburg and I went from online to public school where I met my best friends and got in my first fight. After we moved to Roanoke I got in to sports and nothing changed Until Now.

When my brain finally came back down to earth the car was upside down, and I was dangling from my seat belt. I unbuckled and fell to the ground. I looked out of the whole that was once the windshield to see my parents surrounded by ten people in solid black outfits. They were talking I took the thirty-eight-colt revolver out of the glove compartment. When I looked up my mom was yelling at one of them and then he shot her in the stomach. My dad shot two of them before he was shot in the back twice then fell to the ground. I grabbed the colt, and took aim. All of them died with a single shot to the head after they were all dead I crawled out of the car.

I ran to my mom she looked at me and said "remember I love you polar bear and please take care of your sisters." Then she was turning her attention to the twins who had just gotten out of the car. She called me polar bear something she only said when everything was going wrong.

I ran over to my dad ho looked me in my eyes and said "trust absolutely no one, there is a cabin about two miles from here the passcode is 192142, everything is on the computer in the bedroom baby I love you but you need to go" "I love you dad" I said holding back my tears "I love you too now get out of here" he said. I grabbed his gun and started walking away the twins ran to catch up. We had been walking for about twenty minutes when we saw a dirt trail leading deeper in to the woods. We walked up to the door of this dark green cabin, I punched in the code and went inside. The room was neat furnished with a flat screen and sectional couch with a small kitchen in the corner. I walked around and found the bathroom and garage before I found the bedroom.

I powered up the computer and it asked for a password I tried birthdays, our last name, the code from the door, and their anniversary. Then I asked for a hint and it was your password is INNCORRECT, of course my dad would have a joke even in death. I typed the word correct to find an empty screen except for a single folder entitled Brey. I opened it to find a video and a document, so I clicked on the video and my parent's faces occupied the screen.

"If you are seeing this then you are done with your basic training and you are ready for the next step, but sadly you have to do this on your own. We won't get to see you become the amazing person that you will become, and I want you to know that we will be so proud of you whatever you become," my mom said. "Brey we are sorry we weren't honest with you about what we do, so to set the record straight we don't technically work for the government and we are definitely not spies. Your mother and I eliminate those people who find loopholes and fall through the cracks in the justice system," dad said.

"This is what you need to do" he started "you are going to go to base Naylor and leave the twins where they will receive basic training with Joe Franklin. You will take the final exam and then you will go to a camp which ever one fits you best then you will perfect your craft." "We love you polar bear" they both said then the video ended, and I just sat there crying until I fell asleep. They next morning I opened the document entitled Base Naylor Protocol. The document was fifty-four pages long and included directions to the place, a gate password, a dorm number, and a very long list of rules. I sent a copy to my phone and read a sticky note on the edge of the desk that read in case of emergency this building will self-destruct.

For the next week, the twins and I mourned our parent's death. The news said that we all died in a multi car collision due to a drunk driver. I stopped crying at three that morning just because I didn't want to cry anymore. The next day I woke up at six at night to a loud alarm I went to the computer and it flashed PLEASE EXIT THE BUILDING IN THE NEXT 5 minuets 37 seconds and it started counting down.

The printer was printing off the base Naylor file I grabbed it, yelled for the twins, and ran to the garage. I opened the garage door and pulled off the cover to reveal a navy-blue Chevy Silverado, but no keys I ran back in to the house and tore apart the bed room until I found them. The clock was at 2 minutes 15 seconds when I found the twins asleep on the couch, so I flipped it "WHAT THE HELL" Jazz screamed "we need to go" I yelled back shoving them to the garage. I jumped in to the front seat and started the engine we were a mile away when we heard the explosion. I guess this is my life now I thought looking at the rising ball of fire in the rear view.

I drove for the next hour answering the twins' questions while the sun set, why you, why weren't we trained, did you know, and did our parents know they were about to die. Thankfully we were low on gas after a quick search of the car we found a wallet with four hundred dollars, and a fake

ID with my picture. We went to the nearest gas station, and the twins grabbed some snacks while I pumped.

I looked in the back to find three suit cases and a duffel bag. I opened the duffel and found two Glocks, a revolver, an AR-15, an AK-47, seven magazines per gun, two sets of throwing knives, a katana, and a butterfly sword. The pump clicked, I put the cover on the back of the truck and honked for the twins. We pulled up to our destination to find a gate that read Naylor Ranch, I pressed the button for the intercom, said the password, and the gate opened. We drove up a dirt road to a building, and were met by two large men in grey suits. They grabbed the stuff out of the back and open the door for us to get out of the truck.

"Ms. Rena, it has been forever," the man said who was walking down the stairs towards us. "Who are you," I asked trying to place where I have seen him before. "I'm slightly hurt that you don't recognize me, I'm Joseph Franklin," he said not sparking any memories "you called me Joey," he said reluctantly. "Oh, my gosh," I exclaimed giving him a hug, Remembering that he was my old online school teacher. we followed him inside and we went to dorm 2051 Jazz entered the dorm code and opened the door. Inside was a large living room with a small kitchen off to the side and doors to two bedrooms with JAZZ and JACKIE painted on them. They both grabbed their suitcases and went to their rooms, and Joey told me that my test was tomorrow at eleven thirty.

The next morning I woke up at eight o'clock and took a shower on Jazz's side of the dorm. I washed, conditioned, and flat ironed my dark brown hair that barely touched my shoulders. I looked at myself in the mirror and saw my parents. My dad's chocolate skin, my mom's hazelnut eyes, my dad's nose, my mom's lips, my dad's long eyelashes, and my mom's perfectly styled eyebrows.

I needed to focus, I assumed that this test would have a certain amount of physical activity so I put on a sports bra, gray tank top, leggings, and running shoes. I walked down the corridor at eleven fifteen and followed Joey into a dark room with a metal table, two chairs, and a mirror. I looked at him and he said "all you have to do is not lie and not tell the truth" Then he left the room. Over the next four hours eight people came in and tried to get me to answer their questions. Each of them having a different approach some asking nicely, some threatening my life, some yelling at me, and some even hitting me, but they still all failed. Joey came in and announced that I had passed and broken some record by a long shot.

We walked outside to a huge obstacle course that was about a mile long with a lot of climbing and people standing in for guards. Joe said "Get to the other side and don't let them catch you. You have ten minutes starting now." I sprinted and climbed the first twenty foot Rockwall then jumped down right behind the first guard then grabbed him by the back of his neck and smashed him into the wall. I pretty much continued that cycle climbing, knocking someone out, and running for the rest of the test. When I got to the end Joey said I passed with a perfect score, and I was going to camp Naylor. That night the twins waked me to the car and I gave them one last hug then got in the car and waved goodbye. That was the very last time I cried.

Chapter 2

When my parents died, I was not in their plan, but my brother Zack was until he decided to blindly charge at their killers. My parents were smart enough to train both of us so, when I came to the base alone Joe just made me take the test then and there. I passed my admissions test with a perfect score, and left the same day for camp Naylor.

When I arrived, they took my suitcase and my duffel bag and gave me a tent, sleeping bag, hunting knife, a tee shirt, jeans, and combat boots. I changed and they walked me to a ledge with a zip line leading into what looked like a huge sinkhole. Someone strapped me to it and pushed my off before I could protest. I flew, wind blowing my face, I felt like I was flying, as the ground grew closer I unlatched myself and fell to the ground.

When I stood up I was hit by the stench of burning flesh and greeted by the screams of the dead, tortured, and dying.

I was surrounded by a group of guys who were staring at me like I was their next meal. I grabbed my stuff, then pushed past them, walked to the tree line, and set up my tent in the only place I couldn't hear people screaming.

The next morning I woke up to what sounded like a roaring stadium, but combined with gunshots and screams of agony. Then the roar grew louder, the earth started shaking, and I jumped out of my tent to find a hoard of people charging towards me. I grabbed my gun from my waist band, took aim, and started firing. I shot the first two people in the head, the third in the neck, and another five in the chest before I ran out of bullets. I grabbed my knife and stabbed the first guy who came at me in the stomach, and the next in the jugular. Then I heard shots coming from behind me they shot the guy I was fighting and shot the knife out of me hand. I put my hands up and turned around then saw the girl holding me at gun point.

I asked her not to kill and she just laughed then put down her gun. "Hi I'm Nick" I said "I'm not interested" she said walking away, I for some unknown reason I followed her. "Go away" she said "not until we are even" I replied smiling for some reason. She asked for what and I told her that she saved and spared my life and she replied that she was regretting that already.

I followed her deeper into the woods to a stream that had a fire and a tent beside it. She sat down on a log next to the fire and offered me a seat. I looked around then asked her how long she had been here and she said that she got here yesterday. For the rest of the day we asked each other questions and we both had to answer. I told her about my parents and my brother, and she agreed that he was stupid for doing that.

She eventually told me that her name was Brey and that she had two little sisters also how she killed the people who murdered her parents. I realized that we had spent the entire day talking, and went back to my tent to sleep. When I got there, I stumbled upon people eating the dead bodies that had been sitting there since this morning. I if thought I was hungry wasn't any more I waited until the cannibals dragged the bodies away before I moved my tent then went to sleep.

I woke up the next to a single scream. I jumped out of the tent to watch two of the weirdos from the day I arrived running for their lives from where Brey's tent was. I headed in her direction worried about finding her dead, and became less worried as I passed two guys limping away.

Then became worried for my own safety when I saw one of them crawling away missing both of his legs. When I walked up to her she was cleaning off the knife, and I asked her if she was okay then she looked at me like I had forgotten who she was and answered "Of course." Then I saw the last guy from the group missing both arms and his head. "Are you hungry" she asked holding a can of green beans "Sure" I said surprised that there was another option than other humans. We could chill out until noon when we heard something move behind us.

The first time I heard it thought it was a bird, but the second time she and I knew it was bigger. Brey tossed me her gun and grabbed her knife when a man walked out with his hands up he was about six one with ivory skin, black hair, and almost black eyes. "My name is Chase I'm here to train you both" he started "put down your weapons they won't make a difference."

I put down the gun and Brey put away her knife "If you'd follow me we have some work to do" he said. We crossed the stream and went deeper into the woods until we came to a ladder at the edge of the sink hole. Brey climbed first then Chase then me when I got to the top he took her knife and threw it over the edge. we got in his car and for the next hour we drove in awkward silence with a lot of failed attempts at conversations.

When we arrived at camp Naylor we pulled up to a long school like building with what looked like a race track and a lake behind it and a very large shooting range off to the side. We followed him up two flights of stairs in to a room with a table in the corner, two twin sized beds, two dressers behind them, and a flat screen. "Showers are down the hall to the left I will see you in the morning" he said then left. The first dresser I checked had a drawer full of bras assuming they weren't mine, so I went to the other and got some stuff together for a shower. The showers had nothing special about them like the rest of the place. I washed my hair till it was light brown again and scrubbed my tan skin almost raw. I put on a white shirt and black basketball shorts then went to the room and to sleep.

The next morning was exactly like the next three months wake up at five, running for an hour, long range shooting, hand to hand combat, and breakfast. Then short range, archery and edged weapons training for Brey, and tolerance training where chase either beat the hell out of us, tased us into water, or shot us in the stomach while we wore a bullet proof vest.

Then lunch, motorcycle or Jet Ski training, another round of hand to hand combat but with other groups, then dinner, and afterwards we still had to attend an online version of school. Brey and I became best friends more like siblings, and we could practically read each other's mind. She was always a little more violent and methodical than me, but Chase said that her parents was like that. By the week before the final exam I had forgotten about pain, how to miss, and what losing a fight felt like except for Brey all of those were ties. Everyone knew that if you failed the final exam you either died or went back to the hell hole they called the pit.

On the morning of the exam I woke up to a loud screech and found a trunk at the base of my bed inside were a pair of black jeans, a black shirt with my last name printed on the back, black boots, a helmet, a bow and a quiver of arrows, two Glocks with holsters that hooked to my belt.

Brey was getting dressed as swell but she had a katana and a set of throwing knives instead of bows and arrows. We raced out of the building to find the trainers timing us Cynthia, the training coordinator, said that our time was five minutes we took it as a good sign being the first ones out. We stood there for the next ten minutes watching more people run out of the building before Cynthia made us run four miles to the testing building. When we finally got there, she divided us based on our group there were six on green, five on red, eight on yellow, seven on orange, nine on purple, three on pink, and Brey and I on blue.

Cynthia said to grab a flag from all the other teams from on a motorcycle then blew her whistle to start. First, I grabbed one from pink and yellow, then green and orange, then one from red when they tried to grab mine we stopped when there were eight people left.

We moved on to long and short rage shooting which I aced, then hand to hand which I also aced and Brey broke the other guy's arm after he called her a bitch. Finally, there was the kill test with only Brey and I and two guys from orange named Mark and Eric. Brey and Mark went first after three minutes of shooting, banging, and screaming Mark was rolled out missing his arms, legs, and his head.

Eric and I walked into the room and stood at separate sides of the room until she said to begin. He drew his gun and fired four shots with his eyes closed, and I shot an arrow threw his neck. Brey and Chase walked in while Cynthia took my weapons and whispered "kill her" in my ear I felt sick till Brey looked at me and mouthed the word sorry.

She started off by kicking me in the head then punching me in the stomach, so I pined her arm behind her back and she flipped me. We fought like this for thirty minutes' strait before Cynthia called it a draw. Out of the one hundred forty-seven trainees a camp Naylor only thirty-seven graduated. After Cynthia gave us a very boring graduation speech we all got our fingerprints removed I got my laptop, phone, and smart watch. Then said goodbye to chase and got to the car and headed to the airport.

After I got off my flight and called a car to take me to the hotel. Once I checked my email and I got a note that said that I would have to wait a week before I got any information. There is a total of three camps Naylor where you become an assassin or die trying. Gelna where you could become a hacker, a surveillance specialist, or an automotive and explosive specialist, or Jeatia where you become a spy or also die trying.

The hardest thing was to break my daily routine, but thankfully I saw Brey while she was running one morning and decided to join her. We both did typical tourist stuff getting lost, eating weird stuff, and stalking celebrities. Then when we finally got the team files the first thing I did was check the other assassin and thankfully it was Brey. Our three spies were Hunter Cruz, Emily Sang, and Haleigh Bishop who were all seventeen, were dropped off before the age of seven, and three best at camp Jeatia. Then from camp Gelna Daniel Paul, Justin Anderson, and Victoria Jones.

The next morning I was entered into a group chat with the rest of the members of the team. Apparently, everyone was meeting up for breakfast Brey and I rode there together ate, talked for a little while, and invited everyone to a shooting range. Only Hunter and Victoria or Tori for short came. Hunter was a cool guy he wasn't as annoying as the other two. Tori was quiet and seemed shy she was on her laptop the entire time and Brey seemed to think she was nice.

Victoria was a terrible shot it almost made my cry Hunter helped her a little, but he wasn't the best either at least he hit the target. Brey and I stepped out for a little while and they didn't seem to notice that moment Brey and I made a bet that they would end up dating. The four of us hung out a lot for the next two weeks and as it turns out Tori has a bad side and loves enacting revenge.

One morning I got an order telling to pack my bags and go to the Regale building at ten thirty Tori, Brey, and I rode together. She asked "what did we think we would be doing" "fixing the cracks in the justice system" Brey said sarcastically. When we got there a secretary took us to a board room she shoved Justin and Danny in there after they were flirting with her. After everyone arrived a tall woman with short mint green hair walked in and introduced herself as AG our mission coordinator. She said that our services were required to eliminate a sex trafficking and slavery ring in Missouri she then handed Brey and me a list of names then asked us to start at the top.

Chapter 3

The fight from LA to St. Louis was horrible I almost choked the person in front of me. When it was finally over we met up with AG's contact Caleb where gave us all our gear and gave us all the information he had. Our first few days there we studied them finding out who was in charge, where they kidnapped these women, where their bodies were found, and how old they were.

Then we started focusing on finding a way in the organization Justin proposed the idea of Emily and I getting kidnapped. While Hunter went, and did his own thing Emily and I posed as interns since most of the women found were between the ages of nineteen and twenty-five. A month later we got an apartment down town about two blocks away from our job and continued like normal people. Quick flings, friends, and people we didn't like. After a month with no dice I joined a gym after a week I was kidnapped.

I was walking out of the gym when a green van pulled up and someone pushed me inside. I punched kicked and jerked like I was trying to get away then they put a chloroform soaked cloth on my face and I acted like I passed out. They got on the interstate for about 729 seconds then they turned off, and took two rights and a left.

They dragged me out of the van into a long hallway that felt like it was going on forever we took a left then a right then dropped me in a cage. I laid there for an hour or two then I sat up horrified at the fact that I wasn't alone. I jumped up and ran to the door of the cage screaming for help, for anyone, and I wished this wasn't real fear.

The room was dark the floor was cold and I had no way to get any help they know where I am at least, I thought to myself. Trying to look at my very few positives I started to shake the door to the cage when a whisper told me to shut up. I asked the girl next to me where we were her answer was "HELL" she was terrified, yet when I asked her name she wouldn't stop. Her name was Lana she was from St. Louis like me she had blonde hair and blue eyes and had no clue where she was or how long she had been there.

An hour later three men came in and unlocked the door to her cage, and she rammed him with it, then she sprinted for the door. When he got up he shoot her in the back then kicked her dead body.

The guy with the tablet, who seemed to be in charge, yelled a few cuss words then pointed at me. I pushed myself into the corner and hugged my knees as hard as I could. He opened the door and grabbed me by my hair then dragged me out. He threw me to the ground and kick me in the stomach a few times then rolled me onto my chest and zip-tied my hands. He put a black sac over my head and dragged me out of the room took two lefts and a right then sat me in a chair.

I felt them pull off me jeans and shirt and then a spray of water, so after they finally took the bag off my head and made me put on a black tee-shirt and cut-off shorts. They tied my hair in pony tail then rebound my hands then dragged me into another room when in front of a camera I stood there for five minutes a gun trained at my head. When the guy sitting behind a computer gave a thumbs up and another sack was put over my head then I was dragged away. Then the guy dragging me put something in my pocket and traced the letters HC with his fingernail of course it was Hunter, but I have no clue how he got here. He put me in a car and shut the door.

They drove off and I just sat there with no handles on the inside of the doors. It hurt me that I couldn't do anything to get out of this stupid car, and I hated to have to wait to even see what Hunter gave me. When we finally arrived, the driver pulled me out of the car and into another room then threw me to the ground.

When someone finally took the bag off my head and cut off the restraints I slowly got up. To see a grey-haired man who looked old enough to be my grandfather with a creepy smile on his face. "What's your name my dear," he asked reaching for my arm. I answered him slowly stepping backwards coming closer to the door. "And yours," I asked almost at the door "Edward but you can call me Ed or Eddy," he answered I had finally got my hand on the doorknob, but when I tried to turn it was locked. He then grabbed me by my arm and asked where I was trying to go I answered that I needed to use the restroom. He asked why was I' going to the garage for that I tried to give a little laugh.

He pulled my hand in the bend of his arm, and walked me down a hallway to a grey and white restroom. He told me that I could take a shower if I wanted then shut and locked the door from the outside. I used the toilet and I was washing my hands when I saw the camera I then stepped in the shower, closed the curtain then undressed when I took off the shorts I took the small plastic bag out of the back pocket where I found a receipt for Ed's purchase, a contact lens, and a small earpiece.

I folded the clothes and placed them on the floor then I turned on the shower and looked like I was washing my hair. The second I put in the ear piece Tori, Justin, and everyone else couldn't stop talking. When everyone finally calmed down they basically told me that they were about to blow up the building and bust me out. That moment Ed opened the door and I pretended to be washing my hair he took my clothes and placed a silk nightgown on the counter beside the sink. He called my name and I peeked behind the shower curtain to see something so horrific I was about to puke this eighty something year old man was standing there completely naked.

Tori>> oh god look away, look away, look anywhere else PLEASE

"Do you mind if I join you," he asked

Justin >> YES, YES YOU FUCKIN MIND, oh my god I'm turning this off, their eta is like five minutes, beep.

I told him that I would be out in a second grabbing a towel he then put his robe back on and left the room. I dried my hair, put on the nightgown and the thong he also brought me, and knocked on the door to leave. Ed thankfully clothed this time walked down the hall to a candle lit bedroom with a king-sized bed in the center of the room. He handed me a glass of wine then sat on the bed and I sat across from him taking a few sips of my wine as he talked about how stressful obtaining me was. Tori came back on when he leaned in to kiss me she told me to duck, so I gently laid down on my side right before the glass broke and a bullet drove threw his head.

Tori >> thank you Haleigh for mentally scaring me for the rest of my life

"Well I am sharing the suffering and nightmares with you," I said they told me to shut the hell up. Nick decided that it would be a great idea to crash through a window and Brey being the smarter of the two came through the door with Danny. Who started placing bombs while Nick and Brey started searching the place shooting everyone they found all of them other dirty old men or guards. After they killed everyone we got in the car then started to drive away and Danny blew the charges looking in awe at the ball of fire as we drove away. I felt sorry for all the other girls who had probably been there, all their families, and how great it will feel taking all these assholes down.

Chapter 4

In exactly seven weeks we've had two people get kidnapped, one of them sold and the other kidnapped in the same day. While the other spy went missing for a month then pop up out of nowhere needing Brey and Nick to knock-off a few people, and has needed or wanted Tori to constantly watch his back.

Then there are the chess game killers who have been haunting the people of Branson since we got here with between twelve and twenty people being found dead each week, and a chess board set up with the moves of what looks like a game. The police have absolutely no clue where to even start the second they get a suspect another body is found they don't even have a murder weapon.

Daniel has been bored out of his mind spent his time making small bombs and fixing his car stuff that is remotely productive while Tori was either watching Hunter or hacking random places. Then there's me this sexy, chocolate, breathtakingly handsome guy memorizing everything they do and fixing every mistake they make and believe there is a lot of them.

After we rescued Haleigh we focused on destroying them all at once first we needed a few things to go wrong like all the cops they had in their pocket to be out service or one of the groups of kidnappers to be stopped and there be a few cameras pointed in that direction.

When Tori brought Kecia Webb, a street photographer from St. Louis, and Austin Smith, the son of two lawyers whose parents were recently killed by police officers to life. I didn't think that setting up two assassins might be a little too effective. Two out of three of Kecia Webb's attackers ended up on life support while the other died a very, very, very painful death, and the three officers, four federal agents, and the two other people that were attacked by Austin Smith all ended up in the emergency room together with Austin who had been shot four times.

Brey aka Kecia was sent to a mental health facility because of the extent of her attacker's injuries and that most of them were inflicted by her bare hands. Nick aka Austin was sent to prison for 4 cases of assault on a federal agent, three cases of assault of a police officer, two cases of assault, one case of attempted murder, one case of resisting arrest, and one case of contempt of court. We tried to get them out but they both told us to leave them and that that they will be back.

After we demolished their security net we pushed them off the ledge. First Hunter faked his death then we made an anonymous tip about hearing screaming and that we saw a lot of people with guns around an abandoned warehouse. The FBI took care of the rest with a total of one hundred thirty-eight girls were rescued and one hundred eighty-two people were arrested.

Afterwards AG called us back to LA and we got a First-class flight I guess that is was her way to say thank you. Haleigh and Emily got completely drunk, Hunter and Tori sat and talked the entire time, and while Danny and I hung out with these two girls they were really hot I was surprised that they would even notice us. I don't know what happened, but after about two hours and four drinks we were joining the mile-high club.

When we landed, we went to the hotel and unlike the plane we were cramped they only got two rooms all the girls took one while the rest of us took the other. Nothing really happened Hunter went out with Tori came back and chilled out until the next morning when AG called us in. She told us that we were going home until our next mission, but I didn't know where that was.

My parents live in London and I went there every summer then return for holiday but I wouldn't call that my home I wasn't even paying attention to what she was saying when she handed me a plane ticket. The flight from LA to South Carolina took forever and there were no gorgeous girls on this flight just a lot of older people apparently, there was the class of 1976 high school reunion by the end I felt like I lost a portion of life. When we finally got to the address pulled up to a fucking huge villa right on the water I jumped out of the car to get the keys out of the mail box and read the note team A-214 this is your new living arrangement for now- AG.

I went upstairs the first two rooms were locked I assumed they were for Nick and Brey the next room I checked screamed Barbie it was hot pink with a huge closet I was walking out when Haleigh saw the room and practically threw me out of her way, stood in the center of the room, and screamed.

I backed away slowly then walked down the hall to the last bedroom in the hallway and found a perfect room with a huge TV, an Xbox and bed. I put away my stuff and started up the Xbox I then spent the next four hours on the edge of bed full immersed in the game. Hunter and Tori went out again while Emily and Haleigh went to a local night club. After another hour, Danny and I took some cash from a safe that Emily found and went out as well.

The next morning I woke up at this girl's apartment on the other side of town, but at least I remembered the first few drinks and the girl who I had spent the night with. I called a ride and thankfully left got back to the villa then before Courtney woke up. We didn't stay there for a whole week before we had our next mission and in that's what it was like for the next year with a total of nineteen missions and a total of nine weeks of rest.

After a while AG stopped bringing us to LA and just started popping up on all the TVs then sending us across the country Exton, Midland, Atlanta, Boise, Phoenix, Fitchburg, Glenview, and Warsaw to name a few some missions take a weekend while others take a month. We kept an eye on Brey and Nick as they became two of the top twenty best assassins with a total of 423 kills some out of the country, they joined ARES, a group of the best assassins, hilarious since they were both technically still locked up.

Chapter 5

It was great having Brey back since out of everyone else she is just as quiet as me. She told me everything he did while they were away sparring me the unbelievably gory details. They spent a year practically off the grid then yesterday she and Nick just walk in the front door like nothing happened it could've surprised me. One of the first things I noticed was that they both got tattoos on their left biceps Brey's read DEIMOSA surrounded by a three-inch cascade of butterflies while Nick had a three-inch solid black around his arm with the name PHOBOS in the center.

The day she got back I told her about Hunter and I, and that we haven't really slept in separate rooms for the past two months she seemed happy for me. Then I asked if she and Nick ever hooked up and she screamed hell no, and almost knocked me out with a pillow. The time that she wasn't chilling out with me she would go to this ARES only bar. I don't understand why assassins get these extra perks after they reach a certain level, and why can't there be a group for other professions that get cool perks not like I would join since it sounds too much like a cult.

Brey and Nick had been home for a week before AG popped up on the TV screen scaring Brey half to death. Then she told us that we were going to Orlando, Florida to stop an auction of a flash drive that was leaked from some place that we aren't allowed to know. We left the next morning the flight was very boring and then took a car to where we were staying. The summer bay resort was beautiful it had five pools each one having a small bar next to them.

The other three spies were finding out the details of the auction, but all they knew was that it was going to be in an upcoming art auction. Haleigh was trying to find out what piece the drive would be in and be someone's date to the auction of course. While Brey and Nick were killing most of the other buyers leaving only twenty Danny was helping Brey and Nick get rid of a lot of people's remains and evidence.

Hunter made them stop when they were about to move the date of the auction while I was getting a hold of fifteen of the other buyer's accounts and make them have a sudden money problem. After about a week we devised a plan to get the drive Haleigh was already accompanying Garret

Blevins, Hunter was blackmailing Amelia Clark and Jerod Dasher, while Emily was accompanying Tabitha Philips. Leaving only one buyer left Brycen Holman. Mr. Holman has a very pacific preference in a date height, weight, age, eye color, and skin color. Which only applied to one person in the group and she was not going to do this without some amount of reluctance.

Brey looked stunning in the royal blue dress that Haleigh bought for her and Justin and Danny couldn't stop starring even when she threatened to pluck out their eyes. They all left by the time they got to the gala Brey had already said how she felt stupid ten times. Brey hated being told that she can't do something, so when I said she couldn't just kill the guy she almost left the building.

After Holman started talking to Brey he couldn't stop, and all she did was talk about what she thought was the perfect guy. Everything was going great until they went to one of the hotel rooms upstairs and there was two of his goons waiting for them. Five minutes before the auction started Brey was locked in Holman's hotel room, and everyone else was taking their seats in the auction hall.

The first few pieces to go up were paintings that sold for between two hundred fifty and seventy-five thousand dollars. Then everything got very competitive when they got to the vases most of them dating back to the mid eighteen hundred's. These people spent millions of dollars of these things like they would cure diseases or end world hunger, and not just hold flowers or sit on a wall. When they finally got to the object that was supposed to have the drive in it everyone lost their shit. After the twenty minutes of yelling and people gasping the jewel encrusted power tin sold for twenty-three million seven hundred thousand dollars to none other than Mr. Holman.

Brey was starting to freak out when Holman was walking to the door she was ready to hit him with a vase. When I told her that she couldn't kill him I was naturally surprised when she listened. He walked in pointing a gun at her, and she held up her arms. I kept saying don't repeatedly trying to convince her not to kill anyone while his two body guards patted her down and removed her dress. Holman handed both of his guards some cash and they left the room.

Then started walking towards Brey She took a step for everyone he took forward until she backed into the sofa. He placed his hands on each side of her arms and pulled her closer to him then kissed her "First I would like to apologize for all of this" he started "I have had four of my good friends killed this week, and I'm not used to such an enchanting woman being interested in Me."

Brey tried to pull herself away but he just kissed her again then sat her on the sofa. "How about I make it up to you" he started "I'm going to Venice tomorrow would you like to come with me." I told her to say yes, and He exclaimed

"Great" before kissing her again. Then he poured her a glass of champagne and she started to ask about the art that was sold specially a called a strange dream.

After about an hour or so she fell asleep on the couch, and by that time everyone else was back to witness him do something extremely strange. He took pant and a paint brush from a drawer and started to paint something on her skin. I was hoping that I had just fallen asleep starring at the screen but everyone else reassured my overall confusion. "What the fuck is he doing" Nick started "she's going to kill him."

Brey woke up about an hour after he finished his supposed artwork, and instantly noticed the blue, gray, and white butterfly on her thigh. "Good morning beautiful" he started "how was your rest." "Umm okay I guess" she said still starring and the painting. He then tried at explaining why in the hell he decided to paint something on her, and no matter how much charm he added was still creepy. Luckily someone knocked on the door and brought in a large rack of clothes then left the room.

"So" he started "Since you didn't originally plan to accompany me half way across the world I had someone obtain some clothes for you." He asked her to try on a white and gold sun dress with some solid white shoes, which she of course looked gorgeous in. he kissed her then took her hand and took her to the car waiting down stairs headed for the airstrip. The great part was that he was flying with the artwork that he had just bought including the drive.

Chapter 6

I never realized how hot Brey was I probably didn't notice through all the pony tails, sarcasm, guns, swords, extreme violence, and over all evilness but under all of that she is a perfect ten. After Nick, had snapped the necks of the pilot and copilot I asked him if he had ever had a thing for her.

He admitted that he did but that it ended after he saw her kill a few people with a hair tie and a butter knife. I wanted to ask him how someone would do that but I just didn't want to know or have that image stuck in my head. We got on the plane and waited for them to show up thankfully the pilots had an extra uniform in their bags. One of the pilots was the same size as Nick and the other was about two sizes bigger than me. I tried to get Nick to switch but then Justin started to yell at us to get in the cockpit Then Holman showed up with Brey and two of his body guards.

We had been in the air for about twenty minutes when Tori and Justin gave the okay for me to turn the plane to head to the crash zone, and for Nick and Brey to kill everyone and get the drive. Nick started off by shooting Holman's body guards then he grabbed Brey and put the gun to her head. Next, he said "the drive please" it was strait out of an extremely awesome action movie Brey even added to the nostalgia by pleading for him not to give not to give him whatever it was, but Holman handed it over anyway.

Nick tossed it to me and I sent it to Tori to see if it was real once it checked out Nick shot him in the head. We flew to the area that we planned to crash the plan at, and put the pilots back in their respective seats. Brey sadly changed into a black tee shirt and leggings then we all put on our parachutes, and exited the plane looking unbelievably cool or at least Brey and Nick did I was kind of flailing around afraid I was going to die.

After we hit the ground the three of us to a fun road trip to la only to drop off the drive to AG since she insisted that we deliver it to her personally. I realized that they aren't the best to be stuck in a car with for an extended amount of time I felt like I was trying to talk to two brick walls. Neither of them would say a word so just to try to get any form of communication started me asked if Brey liked her tattoo then she kindly kicked they back of my chair and they both laughed. After we finally gave AG her stupid drive she sent us back home and hoped that we had a peaceful break.

We were at the villa for a record breaking three weeks before AG to give us a mission. We now had to guard a secret uranium vault then find and eliminate all other interested parties, but the catch was that some idiot cleared for a school to be built on top of it. Now the only school in Thomas county Arizona had enough uranium for about forty nuclear warheads and somehow the information slipped out.

So, she had the incredible idea to enroll us as students until the school year was over in three months I have never wanted not to do something so badly, but we still packed our bags and flew to Arizona. Brey and Nick weren't on the same plane as the rest of us since they had to bring some items that weren't exactly legal on a plane.

After we got to the address I felt like I was in a sitcom. There was the mom, Cassie, the dad, James, and their five-year-old daughter Laurel. When a car pulled up to the house we assumed it was Nick and Brey, but then we saw two people doing wheelies down the street. The next day Jonas, May, Emma, Charles, Dominic, Anna, Kecia, and Austin entered Thomas county high school. Because Brey and Nick only have two aliases and the other was twenty-one and was traveled the world while we thought it would be best if certain people avoided them.

The farthest I got in public school was the sixth grade when my parents dropped me off at the base. Where I pretty much did the rest of school on a computer that how I have a Masters in chemistry at seventeen.

The closest I've gotten to the high school experience is high school musical and TV, but Brey told me that all of it was lies "clicks don't exist it's just people and their friends who like to do similar things," she said. My very first day of school consisted of a lot of introductions, getting lost a lot, being bossed around by teachers trying to teach me things I already know, and having to be clueless about what to do. After three days, I have pretty much given up on all of this stuff and started pissing off everyone with Justin who was in every class with me.

After we got home Cassie made us do our homework, keep our room clean, and help make dinner She reminds me of what very I remember of my mom before she dropped me off at Naylor. Out of the eight of us four of us are orphans Tori whose mom was shot and drove her, her sister, and her two older brothers seven hours to the gates of base Naylor Tori was twelve. Brey and Nick's parents were set up and killed by a firing squad, but Brey killed all of them.

Then there's me two years after my parents dropped me off I got a letter saying that they were dead. While the other four's parents are alive and well inviting them over for the summer, sending happy birthday and post cards, and calling them on Christmas. They all have other siblings who they barely talk to, or avoid all together since they feel like they were just ditched then replaced.

About a week after we showed up everyone pretty much found a place they felt like they belonged. Brey or Kecia was the girl that no one messed with or you ran the chance of being in the ER in the week that we have been here she has already almost killed four people.

Haleigh or Emma is nice and hot in other people's opinion and currently has at least two boyfriends, she gets invited to every party, and is in everyone's business. Emily or May is even worse about being in everyone's business and a full fledge instigator. Jonas was really quiet but still talked in class and stuff while Tori or Anna is completely silent, but no one thought she could talk people started to pick on her and Brey threw them down the stairs. Justin and I or Dominic and Charles in detention more than class thankfully.

Then there is Nick or Austin who every girl won't shut up about if I hear "are you friends with him; does he have a girlfriend" one more time I will probably snap I don't get why all the girls are swooning over him since I'm single. After a month, we started to have normal teenage problems. Getting grounded for not keeping our room clean, getting detention, sneaking out to go to parties, or missing curfew. Luckily for Brey and Nick they were sent their list of people to eliminate then they started to disappear.

Chapter 7

I was a normal girl who had good grades in school, a normal family, and a normal job until the day Austin Smith walked into my biology class and life changed. He is the cutest, hottest, sweetest, guy I have ever met. He is so shy it's adorable he just wants to be left alone.

He seems really mean to everyone else, and teachers hate him because he already knows everything. He seems to always be looking for a fight and bluntly doesn't care what people think of him, but he does like me. He has short light brown hair, gorgeous green eyes, and he looks like a Calvin Klein model.

In the month since he first spoke to me he has been really nice and to most of the other girls in the school. Sadly he seems to be easily aggravated leading him to get in to a few fights that didn't end well for the other guy, and making me almost want to avoid him. When I asked my mom for advice she said that it was an extremely bad idea and that I shouldn't even try.

Austin really seems to like me he always talks to me whenever he sees me in the hall and whenever he had to pick a partner in biology he would pick me. I have butterflies in my stomach whenever he says a word to me and I get a chill down my spine whenever he touches my hand.

I'm so lucky I have gym with Austin all I can think of most of the time is how hot he looks in a muscle shirt, but he is very competitive especially with his foster sister Kecia who is a complete psycho that practically lives in the guidance counselor's office. During our karate unit, they almost killed each other and I was ready to kill her if she hurt him, but when they were done they acted like nothing happened. I asked her in the locker room if they dating or trying to date and she said "NEVER in a TRILLON years, that's like insist."

The next unit was dance and Mr. Pope let the girls pick their partners and whichever girl finished their warmups first got first pick. I knew ten out of the twelve girls in the class wanted to dance with Austin and Kecia wouldn't chose him and Rachel was dating May, Austin's other foster sister. Right before we started coach Pope decided to up the ante by saying that the winner gets fifty bucks then blew the whistle to start the one mile warm up and we took off Austin and Kecia were in front for the entire mile which only took them like five minutes David, Ashley, Antonio, and I were two laps behind them I tried to pass Ashley and she pushed me into the wall.

The room was spinning for what felt like forever I tried to lift myself up then Austin was standing there helping me up Mr. Pope was yelling at Ashley and I was totally done with her it's just a race she was taking it way to seriously. "You okay," he asked I nodded my head "she must have wanted to dance with you really badly," I said. He laughed "well that's stupid," he said I asked why and he said "why would I show up to dance for the entire class."

I felt so stupid for thinking out all the people in the class he would even show up for this, so I asked him if he hated dancing and he answered "gorgeous I am probably the best dancer you have ever met but I'm not doing that" "well that doesn't make you the best then," I said walking to the rest of the group where Ashley was yelling at Kecia about how it's her fault that she pushed me.

Ashley Tran is the most annoying, evil, conceded, two faced person in the whole school and I like most people hate her, but no one was stupid enough to yell at Kecia Webb not even teachers. Ashley realized where that was going when everyone moved from behind her and turned her attention to me storming towards Austin and I. "you need to stop being so overdramatic" she started "calm down it was just a race" I replied "well I guess you don't care if I pick Austin as my partner," she said. Austin just laughed and said "really" "yes really" she yelled back Austin's alarm went off then he did something I would never have expected he kissed me on the cheek and said "I'll pick you up at eight babe" I practically exploded.

Chapter 8

That night I was sitting at home then I heard the doorbell when I looked out my window and saw his motorcycle outside. I sprang out of my bed and changed as fast as I could into a dark blue dress, black leggings, and black ankle boots. My mom walked in while I was putting on my makeup "Chloe please tell me that the guy that's down stairs isn't the same Austin Smith that we were talking about you not dating" she started.

"Sorry mom, can you stall him for like twenty minutes" I answered "Chloe Alyssa Price, he is a convicted felon, with a very violent record" she said "mommy he is so sweet and smart and funny you'll like him" I said mocking a baby voice. I looked at myself one more time before she and I went down stairs I looked sweet and pretty.

I went downstairs and he gave me a helmet which I didn't even know he owned since he never wore one. My dad asked him where his was and Austin said that he didn't need one. Then my dad gave Austin his speech on how he would track him down to the ends of the earth if he needed to. He helped on the back of his bike and I wrapped my arms around his waist. He smelled like leather, soap, and a really nice cologne.

I was trying to focus on not rubbing his abs which was a rock hard six pack. Then we finally left the entire time Austin was a perfect gentleman he let me pick the movie, where we went to eat afterwards, paid for everything, and held every door open for me. There was only one thing that was troubling me how could this sweet, nice person sent nine people to the ER, so I asked putting our entire date in jeopardy. To my surprise, he told me he said two rookie cops killed his parents and older brother by overreacting during a sobriety test and he got really drunk then tried to get revenge.

When I got home that night I couldn't stop thinking about him. The next day he called me I don't know why I was so nervous and I sounded so stupid. He was too busy laughing at my nervous nonstop talking to catch all the weird stuff I was saying, and all I wanted was to be able to shut up. After I could stop and put some duct tape over my mouth he asked if I wanted to grab something to eat later and I practically ripped my lips off to say yes. I tried to play it off like I didn't feel like I could fly then I told him to pick me up around two.

After I hung up and found my mom and dad standing in the doorway staring at me. "Chloe I'm a bit worried about you dating a guy with a criminal record" my dad said bluntly "We just don't want you to get hurt" my mom started "So if you are going to keep spending time with him we are going to need to know where you are at all times" she said handing me a small chip " it's a tracking device and from now on I want you in this house by eleven and you need to call me if you are going to be running late." I agreed to their terms. "So where are you two going and what are you wearing" she said excited while my dad just rolled his eyes and walked off.

By the time two rolled around my mom and I had gone through six outfits, five hair styles, and three full faces of makeup. We settled on jean shorts, a floral crop top, a black vest, with a silver choker, and matching earrings. Austin arrived at the door exactly on time upon ringing the doorbell my dad and brothers answered it. Mike and Jonathan aren't every small people they're both six thee and go to the gym religiously, while my dad kept himself in shape by running and lifting weights in the basement. By the time, I could walk downstairs they had already surrounded him, and mom, my sister Heather, and I had to break up the stare down. By the time, Austin and I made it out of the house his life had been threatened at least twenty times.

He took me to a little overlook near the Peak of Mingus Mountain where we had a perfect view of the entire county and we had a picnic. We had been talking for a while aka me unable to stop rambling when he just reached out and kissed me. I felt the entire world melt away for just a moment like nothing mattered not school, not my overprotective family, not even the bug that was crawling on my ankle. When he leaned away from me I felt like I was being snatched back to earth. He smiled at me and brushed my hair back behind my ear and said that had wanted to do that ever since he walked into the school. I kissed him again rolling him on his back and from that day forward that little overlook near the Peak of Mingus Mountain became our little get away.

About three weeks later was the first time he beat someone up on my account. I work as a waitress at a sports bar, and I have gotten to drunk and rude customers being a bit aggravating. One day I had Austin to pick me up from work since my brothers, dad, and Heather were out of town on a case and my mom was at work. It was almost the end of my shift and this one customer was being a big asshole, and had already cussed out two other waitresses before I was forced to wait on him.

Austin arrived early and was sitting at a booth in the corner, and I was bringing the customer his last drink and the check and apparently, he wasn't happy about the price of everything he had ordered. He slapped me to the ground a started to cuss me out while Austin was helping me off the ground and while my boss was kicking him out. After Austin made sure I as okay he walked outside to confront the customer the guy said something, and Austin proceeded to beat the hell out of him. Then he walked back inside leaving the other guy knocked out in the street and received the applause from the other men in the bar then he gave me a ride home. The next morning the news said that the man was hit by a car and was in the hospital.

At school I became the girl with the crazy boyfriend, but I also kept him out of a lot of fights and he got detention a bit less since he wanted to spend more time with me. He was still one the schools' crazy students and he did beat up anyone who called him that. He got into a lot of trouble when he punched Ashley Tran after she had kissed him, so much he was forced to be in the schools anti-bullying play.

Where he was forced to play the kid, who stood up to his bully and his acting is extremely terrible since he was just reading the lines he wrote on his arm. His foster siblings got a real kick out of it especially his roommate Jonas who is also his second-best friend besides Kecia. When he finally invited me over for dinner Jonas, Kecia, and Anna where the only people he willingly introduced me to since he didn't seem to like the other four. After a while I finally convinced him to have dinner with my family, and he was a Perfect gentleman and even brought a bottle of wine. It took two months for my brothers and dad to stop threatening to kill him.

Chapter 9

I felt like I knew almost everything there was to know about Austin, but there was something else that he wasn't telling me. The next week he and Kecia started disappearing when I asked him where he was going he said it was better for me not to know. Then he just stopped showing up, whenever I tried to go somewhere with him he said that he had to go do something, and Ashley was talking about how he was avoiding me.

When he finally resurfaced and everything went back to normal I asked him if his secret mission was over, and he answered no without even thinking then he tried to play it off like it was a joke. I asked him if he was a spy and he said no trying to hold back laughter. "Okay Mr. Smith or do you prefer agent" I replied "I Promise you I'm not a Spy" he said laughing. "Your Right you would probably be an Assassin" I said. He asked why I would think he would be an assassin, and I gave him a list of reasons why I thought he would be one. Then he just kissed me and I walked into my class.

Later that night he called me and of course I answered at first everything was muffled I guess he called me by accident. I was about to hang up when I heard "I DON'T KNOW HOW SHE FIGURED IT OUT" Austin screamed "IF I DID I WOULD TELL YOU." "Dude stop screaming you know exactly what you need to do" another voice said "we just need to eliminate the problem."

"I can't do that" Austin said "well why not" the other person said then a pause "no" the other person said laughing "Is Nick Smith the very person who said that love is a divine form of control in love?" "What would be the fucking problem with that" Austin replied "then you would be a hypocrite" the other voice answered. "I'm not saying that I'm in love but I don't want to kill her, I enjoy her company, I hate ditching her, and I feel attached to her" he replied.

"One that was pretty much the dictionary definition of love, two Romeo I'm so sorry that your Juliet was smart enough to figure out your very bad charade, and I'm sorry that you need to kill her so she doesn't get kidnapped or tortured or did you want that to happen." "Of course, not" he answered "all we have to do is kill her painlessly and not blow our cover." I hung up horrified that Austin was going to kill me when he called me back I told him I was grounded and avoided him for the next three days.

My dad told me not to touch his computer unless it was an emergency, so I opened his database and entered everything I knew about Austin male, six one, green eyes, brown hair, between ages seventeen and twenty. I was expecting thousands of names but there were only about seven hundred. Thirty of which had the last name smith then I entered his name as an alias leaving me with ten other people and assassin Nick Westley Smith.

His parents were killed by a mercenary firing squad were his older brother Zack was also killed. He was trained by Chase McFry along with Brey Z. Rena, who killed the same mercenary firing squad after they killed her parents. They each currently have three hundred fifty-six confirmed kills and over fifty-seven successful assignments he is even an assignment right now.

Then Austin or Nick or whatever his name is called me "Hey is everything okay" he started I told him I was FINE then he said "Are you sure because you sound pissed" "I don't know Nick why would I be pissed" I blurted then he hung up. My dad walked into the room and asked "what's wrong" I told him everything he took the laptop then asked me if I was sure that he was the right person with a look of absolute fear. "Chloe please tell me that he doesn't have any tattoos" he said "yeah he has one on his arm but what does that matter" I replied. "Chloe that means that he is an extremely dangerous person that is probably on his way here." He said calmly trying to hide the panic in his voice. I asked him how he knew all of this, but just before I could finish my sentence the doorbell rang.

Chapter 10

Dad went downstairs and told Austin that he should leave, but He kept telling my dad that he needed to talk to me. I walked down stairs to find an entirely different person standing there, and this boy looked menacing wearing a solid black shirt and jeans. With a gun on one side and a hunting knife on the other.

"I don't want another lie" I said "I promise you that I will not lie to you anymore" he answered. "Well then tell me" I said "I am definitely not doing that here" he replied I told him that I'm not going somewhere for him to kill me "I'm not going to kill you" he responded rolling his eyes. He tossed me a helmet and I got on the back of his motorcycle and we rode to our little spot near the peak of Mingus Mountain.

"What did you lie to me about" I started "a lot" he answered. "Did you actually go to prison" I yelled at him, He calmly said yes, "did you beat up those people," "yes." "Are your Parents and Brother Dead," "yes." For the next hour, I just stood there asking what was and wasn't a lie and I was so mad, but not at him for lying at me for forgiving and believing him. I was mad that I was starting to trust him, and when I was done interrogating him I found myself feeling safe in his arms. Then I asked him if he loved me and he whispered "yes" in my ear, and I couldn't stop myself from kissing him. Then I heard someone pull up, felt a sharp pain in my side, heard a bang, and everything went black.

I woke up on a dusty couch, Austin I mean Nick and Kecia were loading their guns, and I had a huge headache. I moaned and Nick finally looked up "good morning beautiful" he said lifting me up. He gave me a kiss on the cheek then pulled me up my side was burning "what happened" I asked "what do you remember" he countered. "A really loud gunshot" I answered "sorry" Kecia called out from the corner. "Oh, by the way this is Brey she is pretty much my Robin" he said "Don't lie to yourself, I am definitely Batman" she replied playfully. I asked how long was I out Brey said "like three days" while Nick said "an hour at most." They both got a notification on their phones then Brey grabbed some stuff from the table and left the room, and I asked Nick what was going on then he said that my parent were on their way here.

Three minutes later my mom, dad, brothers, and sister burst into the room all their guns aimed on Nick. "Chloe get away from him" dad said "dad calm down" I said "honey he has killed at least eighty people since he has got here" mom said walking closer to Nick. He turned to me and said "it's not eighty its forty-five at best" "see he admits it" she yelled. Nick snatched her gun out of her hands, unloaded it, and tossed it on the couch. Mike and Heather were ready to kill him right there, but I tried to calm them down by explaining what was going on. Everything started calming down, and I was trying to get my family to put away their guns. Mike and Heather holstered theirs first then my dad, and just as Johnathan was starting to move Brey walked in and Jonathan fired two shots at her.

Brey threw a knife in his shoulder then walked over and threw him to the ground. She beat the hell out of him everyone tried to get her off him she knocked out Heather and Mike in the process and threw a knife in his other shoulder. By the time Nick finally got her to calm down she had given my dad a bloody nose that was probably broken. "Y'all need to go" she said "We're not going anywhere without Chloe" my mom said Then we heard a few people pull up. Brey pushed me in to a small room and pushed the rest of my family in there with me then shut the steel door. It was so dark and smelled like rust then I heard someone come in and he and Nick started talking then the shooting started there was a loud banging on the steel door then blood started seeping from under it after about five minutes of shooting we heard someone start screaming then complete silence.

Nick opened the door and put his arm on my shoulder and walked me out of the building shielding my eyes with his huge bicep. He took me to my parent's car and as always opened the door for me my parents walked to the car then drove off. I asked them my dad why his computer had a database full of spies and assassins Heather said "Put it together Chloe." The entire ride home my loving family were explaining that they were all spies and why the kept it from me and I wasn't really surprised. The next morning I woke up and I saw everything a bit clearer and continued like everything was normal. That weekend Nick took me to the rest of his family; Hunter, Nick's roommate and best friend besides Brey, his girlfriend Victoria or Tori who was a computer genius and so sweet. Haleigh who reminds me of Reese Witherspoon in legally blonde but not as rich, Emily is a true extrovert who Nick thinks is bossy. Then there was Justin who Nick described as bossy and annoying and Daniel who was just annoying, but I thought they were both funny.

I finally asked Nick a question that had been bothering me "what did you have to do to get out of killing me" I asked instantly regretting it. "I owe ARES a favor" he answered

I asked him who Ares was and he said "a huge group of major assassins that I'm a part of." I asked him what he had to do "I don't know I hope it's not something too crazy" he said "define too crazy" I said. "To get in I had to kidnap a FBI agent, get caught, get released, get arrested, break out, and then get the charges dropped all in two weeks" he answered "Okay" I said not knowing how to reply. "You do know you can't tell anyone about this" he said "I kind of figured that" I replied. Before going home, I asked him one last question "so what happens to me after your mission is over" "my love if you don't break up with me you may be stuck with me for a while" he answered He kissed me and it was the most amazing feeling in the world and I thought if this was the rest of my life I would be a very happy person.

Chapter 11

Since I was five I have wanted to be the popular girl at school and thanks to this mission I have met my lifelong dream and met the love of my life Rachel she is so smart and super funny, and I wish there was a way that I could tell her the truth about my family like Nick can but I can't. Whenever I think of leaving her I start wishing I had never started talking to her, and avoided the immense amount of pain that I'm going to feel knowing that I will never see her again.

After my class with Rachel I volunteer in the office where I try to keep everyone on task the people in the office think Brey needs to be on medication or in a strait jacket. Every time there is a second of hope she almost kills someone, and it doesn't help that Mr. Pope lets and encourages for Nick and her Spar in gym class. Thankfully Nick calmed down after he met Chloe, but there are those times he gets sent to detention for sleeping in class or throwing someone down the stairs. Danny and Justin get sent to detention at least once every day for disrupting class, yet Haleigh, Hunter and Tori have flown below the radar.

The vault hasn't been touched the entire time we have been here, but there has been a lot of people who have tried. Brey and Nick killed a lot of people trying to avert other interested parties causing Tori to need to change people's minds and erase information. One group is left and they talk about how they'll go for it when absolutely no one expects it, when we told AG and she said to be ready for an attack at all times. Next week the least number of students would be there because Thomas county high school only required failing students to take exams and next week was exam week. I thought it was a bad idea to let Brey have all her toys with her, but I forced to shut up when an assault rifle was shoved in my face.

I put my hands up and slowly tried to stand up then my teacher moved in front of me and was shot for it Mr. Humphrey fell to floor blood pooling from his back. I grabbed my bag then they forced us into the gym after being there for about four seconds I heard someone say "HOLY SHIT THERE IS A BOMB IN HERE." I couldn't breathe for a total of five seconds trying to think of what I needed to do, and thankfully Haleigh came up with a plan first.

Haleigh> "okay Nick, Brey, and Tori go protect the vault. Danny diffuse the bomb. While the rest of us will get everyone out of here"

Hunter> "yeah that works"

Brey> "why don't we all go protect the vault that's the reason we're here"

Tori > "WHAT!!"

Nick > "but you won't blow your covers and no witness"

Chloe> "NO!!!"

Me> "Brey and Nick Go kill these assholes while the rest of us follow Haleigh's plan"

Brey> "fine, but I'm killing anyone who annoys me"

Justin> "deal"

Crazy one and two took Tori and picked the lock to the girl's locker room and rushed to the vault. While Haleigh tried to get everyone's attention and finally got it after wasting bullets on the ceiling and started her speech. "Everyone listen up" she started "I'm Asia Nash from the department of homeland security, and right now my team and I's main priority is to get all of you out of here." Everything was going great until Ashley Tran opened her fucking mouth "Bullshit" she started "your probably with these assholes" I don't know how but she got everyone to believe her and in five minutes somehow, we were tied up in the corner and Chloe was tied up getting yelled at by half a dozen people. They took Haleigh's phone and texted Brey and Nick that there was a problem in the gym.

When Brey showed up Ashley should have realized that it was a bad idea to Point a Gun at Brey Rena, and an even worst idea ambushing her. When Brey entered the gym the first three people to rush at her were stabbed and one got their throat cut the next five were even dumber each getting a bullet to the head or a slashed throat. Then she got to Ashley who Brey said she wanted to kill on day one. First, she untied Chloe and made her hold her weapons them she walked over to her. Ashley was stupid enough to swing on her, Brey grabbed her by her arm and beat the shit out of her figuratively and literally then Brey snapped her neck. Chloe untied us then Brey walked over and let us know that she was right took her swords and guns from Chloe and went back to whatever she was doing.

We told everyone that Ashley was sent as a plant years ago, and then we forced everyone into a small room in an underground corridor near the vault. Danny and Chloe diffused the bomb with three minutes left, and ten minutes later Nick and Brey said everyone was dead. We called AG and she completely understood and had all the witnesses sent to the Keymore facility somewhere in Canada.

That was the last time AG would ever think of letting any of us near a school ever again. When we got back Brey disappeared for a few days and Nick and Chloe kept going out a lot. While I did very important things like Channel, Gucci, Fendi, Jimmy Choo, and Louis Vuitton. After Haleigh and I came back from our hours of shopping we went to lunch. The next morning, we saw Brey and Nick leave for their morning run, and we went to Dino's. When we walked into the house we found Chloe tied up on the floor knocked out then I saw a huge fist coming at me.

I woke up tied to Haleigh and gaged with Danny and Justin were tied up next to us and Chloe was still knocked out on the staircase. The guy who knocked us out was sitting on the couch starring out the window he was about six one with black hair, ivory skin, and black eyes.

We heard Brey and Nick coming up to the door when the opened it Nick went over to Chloe. Then the guy cleared his throat, and Brey hurled a knife at his neck. To my complete amazement, the dude caught it inches from his neck he smiled at her and said "that was actually close" tossing the knife on the couch. Brey walked over and hugged him while Nick had finally woken up Chloe. Nick introduced her to the stranger "This is Chase, he pretty much taught me everything I know." "So you're the girl that Nick can't live without" he started "it's nice to meet you." The four of them talked for a while then Brey and Nick Both packed a bag and told us that they would be back in a week.

After about ten more minutes Hunter and Tori walked in and noticed that we were still tied up. The next day AG gave us a mission, but she said that Tori was not allowed to come with us for some unknown reason. Tori was still on the mission but neither she nor Chloe could leave the Villa. When we left the next day two huge body guards plus two other agents arrived and said they were there to watch them. Hunter kissed Tori goodbye and promised Tori that he would be back then he finally got in the car.

Chapter 12

The whole reason that Chase was here was because of Chloe, and the only reason she is here is because of a deal that he was here to collect on. Chase was focused on one thing and that was getting his wife Abby and their unborn child back who was kidnapped by some of his former friends, and was trying to get me out of the deal I made with ARES as well.

We drove all the way to Salem Virginia just for him to get back to his house to call them. We heard the voices of at least five different people and he heard the voice of his wife Abby in the back cussing someone out. He demanded that his wife be put on the phone they complied, and she was crying begging for him to leave her and move on like that was going to happen. We heard some cars and a motorcycle pull up then someone running to the door, and by the time chase hung up the house was surrounded. Brey and

I started having her version of fun by decapitating a total of fifteen people leaving one person alive.

Out of all the times we have needed information from someone Brey has gotten it and whether that person is dead or requiring decades of therapy is usually up to them. This poor soul was thrown through a window and was screaming for mercy before he even tried to lie to her. She is completely insane to the one hundredth power, and it kind of scares me a little how the she can just attach all her anger to one person to a point that she wants to kill them. She kicked him and threw him a few more times before he told her where they were hiding Abby at 2051 Dansbury drive then Brey finally put a bullet in his head. Brey called a cleaning service for the bodies, and we tried to come up with some form of plan of how we were going to try to get her back.

We settled on Brey going in through the basement and killing a few people in the process of finding Abby because that was probably where they were keeping her. While chase and I get in the house from the front and back door and finishing off the rest worst case scenario we all die. Brey broke in threw a window into the basement and killed everyone, but she didn't find Abby I did when she hit me in the head with a vase. Instead of hiding her in the basement they had locked her in the bathroom which was my second guess, but I wasn't expecting the vase it didn't knock me out it just dazed me a bit. I grabbed her by the arm, drug her out the house, shoved her in the back of Chase's car, and drove off with Brey and Chase in her car.

"Who are you" she asked "Nick" I answered "what do you want" she asked almost crying. "a burger" I answered really considering stopping to get something to eat "do you want one" I asked she shook her head no "okay if I want a burger I have to just deal with just it, but if you want a burger I have to get you one, so you want a burger right" I explained to her and she still said no. "Where are you taking me" she asked crying "not to get a burger" I said sarcastically. "My husband is going to kill you" she yelled "no he's not" I said rolling my eyes "yes he is" she spat back at me. I called Brey and put her on speaker "what" she answered "how wrong would it be if taped her mouth shut" I asked "very" they both yelled. "Sorry I'm hungry" I said "that's not a good reason" Chase said "well she said you were going to kill me" I said "I'm thinking about it" he replied.

Brey started laughing then he said "don't think you're not on the chopping block too Rena" "that's not funny" she said. "So, where I am going" I asked "we are following you" Brey answered "well I'm getting something to eat" I yelled then hung up. I pulled up at a burger king and practically had to drag Abby inside. When Chase got there, she ran to him and they had a very romantic moment, and I ordered two whopper combo meals with an extra order of chicken fingers.

Chase had apparently told his wife about us because when he introduced us to her she said that she understood why he tased me then we all sat down and ate together like a weird family. Abby asked about Chloe and I told her about how great she was, and then I started missing her then I thought about how she is probably at the villa bored out of her mind. Then to my amusement Abby asked Brey if she was with anyone and she answered no, and Abby asked why Brey said that it was because she couldn't find the right person then tried to change the subject.

Afterwards Brey drove us home for the entire drive I was either sleeping or thinking about Chloe. When I walked in the door to my bed room she was laying on the bed in one of my hoodies. I didn't want to wake her so I went and took a shower and she was standing in the doorway when I got out and she almost knocked me over kissing me. I picked her up and walked over to the bed I ran my hand through her hair. Kissing her felt like the closest I would probably get to heaven.

I sat down on the bed and she pushed me on to my back and she grab me by the back of my neck kissing me deeply, slowly, passionately like she wanted me right then right there. I kissed her back just as passionately holding her against me tightly. My hand drifted up her back to undoing her bra as we kissed her I slipped off her panties quickly rolling her on her back and climbing on top of her. Time seemed to slow down with every kiss, touch, and breath with each time I pulled closer to her a new kind of ecstasy surged in the space between us.

The next morning I woke up with head laying on my shoulder and I just laid there trying to understand how this girl would love me of all people. This girl with light brown hair that came to her back, amazing hazel eyes, and soft sun kissed skin even wanting to be around me is surprising. She woke up, looked at me and I said "good morning gorgeous" she just smiled and kissed me. For the next five weeks AG sent Brey and I on a few hits, but none of them took more than a few days. Chloe decided that she wanted to go back to school and become a real estate agent, so she didn't feel like she had no life except for when I was home. Tori was getting worried about hunter but he did call a few times to hear her voice or to get her to do something for him.

A few days later we were having a normal morning Tori was sitting on the couch reading a book, Brey was watching a movie, Chloe was doing homework, and I was making breakfast. When hunter popped up it was at the most interesting part of Brey's movie and she told him to call back later and to hang up. Apparently, he was in serious trouble and really needed Tori to open a door for him and get him three plane tickets home. I asked what happened he said he couldn't explain it right now then hung up the second the door opened. For the next eighteen hours Tori was pacing next to the front door going hysterical we tried to calm her down, but with every hour she hadn't heard from him made her panic more. Thankfully, he walked through the door before she completely lost it, but only Emily and Justin were with him.

Chapter 13

I don't know what happened two days ago, everything was going smoothly we made our plan to get the weapon and get the hell out of here, but none of us would have ever thought that Danny would do this to us. Thankfully, Hunter could get the others and the weapon out in time, but I'm still trapped in this dam house.

I really hope that Hunter isn't going to blame himself for not seeing that Danny would ever become the traitor that he is. I keep trying to think about the two positives that I have Danny hasn't sold me out and that they don't have the weapon. I completed the mission and that's all that matters, but the second I see Danny I'm going to punch him. The fact that he was so easily bought hurts I thought we were at least friends and now not only is he following their orders, but he seems to be happy even proud about what he did to us.

I'm stuck here in my cute bikini serving them their drinks and being forced to act like I'm giving the nasty men that come in my room a night something other than a laced drink and the pleasure of waking up next to me. I hate this place that sole purpose is to objectify women as toys and I'm pissed at the fact that all Danny wanted was two million dollars and a pass to come to this place went ever he wants.

I can't wait until one of them realizes that he was one of us and kills him because of it. I need to find a way of getting out of here before AG finds out that Danny works for them now knowing what little he does about the group we work for. He thinks it's an excellent idea to do whatever they say just because they pay him, but doesn't realize how expendable he is making himself after he destroys all their enemies.

Now I need to focus on a way to break out of here before AG sends a missile or something. A week after Hunter escaped with Justin and Emily there have been these two guards that seem familiar to me they are twins and about seventeen. I can't see their faces all I can tell is they seem kind of muscular and are blonds. I wanted to bring it up but didn't at the same time since they are probably on a mission which could be to rescue me. They seemed protective of me not that I minded having someone helping me since I was running low on drugs. After shift was over I was still on my own one of the guys I knocked out had his phone on him and I called AG who told me that I was going to be evacuated and that Brey and Nick had been Ordered to take care of Danny.

When I heard the alarm, I knew it was Brey and Nick. Then the two guards outside the door pushed me against the wall and injected me with something and I passed out. My mind went back to one of the summers I spent with my parents in Wisconsin. I'm the middle child of five my two older sisters Carrie and Amanda, me then my two younger brothers Max and Aaron. I barely remember Amanda and Carrie since we only met a few times, but Max, Aaron, and I were all dropped off at the same time and shared a room.

I haven't talked to them since I took the admissions test which was three years ago, and I feel guilty about it. I remember me promising that I would try to keep up with them, but sadly I didn't and I'm starting to regret it. When I returned to Earth I was laying in the backseat of a car. The sun was warming my face I tried to open my eyes, but it felt like the sun was inches from my face. I rolled on to my back trying to ease the extreme headache I had, and my pounding heartbeat didn't help, but I realized it wasn't just my headache.

The first time I asked to stop blaring whatever it was that they were playing my loving brothers turned it even louder, but after kicking the back of Max's chair a few times he finally turned it off. "So" Max started "how have things been going" I laughed and said "okay."

I asked them what I had missed then Max unloaded the past three years of events in around three minutes, and all I could catch was that Max became a spy, Aaron became an assassin, their original teams are all dead, something about kangaroos, Aaron was kick threw a window, and that AG sent them. I really didn't want to ask anything else except I had no idea where I was and where we were going so I asked, and they said that they were following Nick and Brey which didn't make me feel better. Then I started hearing the screaming from the trunk and all they did was turn back on the music I would've been mad but I loved the song that was playing.

When we finally stopped to get something to eat Nick knocked Danny back out and tossed a bag of chips back there. Then we stopped at this diner for lunch or breakfast or whatever meal it was. Aaron was being oddly quiet I was about to say something when Brey said something to him. I don't know what she said to him, but it made him a lot more sociable almost like his normal self. After a few more hours of driving we got on a helicopter and flew to LA, and took Danny to AG. I was feeling bad for him until he said that I was a complete idiot for risking my life for nothing. I won't know what he means by nothing, but I've risked my life shutting down sex trafficking rings, stealing weapons technologies that could kill millions, and demolishing crime rings.

After we arrived at AG's office she looked at him with so much hatred as if she wasn't the one smiling at him and telling him that he was doing great. She had Nick and Brey drag him into another room and lock the door. She walked over to a large chair and sat down, and Max, Aaron, and I sat on the sofa across from her. "First off I would like to say that you handled everything extremely well" she started "in light of Mr. Paul's disloyalty we are to investigate to see if the rest of you have been compromised." We heard Danny start screaming and then stop suddenly "I don't handle betrayal very well" she said with a smile. Nick and Brey walked out of the room each with a cloth wiping off their hands both smiling, so when AG asked them if they left Danny alive Brey answered "yes" trying not to laugh while Nick said, "he just in excruciating pain" sarcastically.

"Also" AG started "your time in conditional housing is over meaning that it's time for you to move out. You will be given an office space and a personal paycheck for you to spend as you wish. This has nothing to do with the actions of Daniel and these changes will be after the investigation." When she finished telling us everything I only had three questions where are we moving to, when this investigation is going to start and end, and what are Aaron and Max going to be doing.

AG said that Aaron and Max had another assignment to get on then shoved us out of her office and onto a flight home. The people AG sent to interrogate us were incredibly thorough and asked all of us a lot of questions, and it was hard for me to sit in an interrogation room and tell the truth. They talked to Justin for longer than anyone else then asked him to try to remember all of Danny's ex-girlfriends, flings, and one night stands let's just say that he couldn't. When they talked to Chloe I could tell that Nick was nervous, but then they were done talking to her she was perfectly fine. They took all of Danny's things then left, and after they were gone it felt like Danny never existed. After AG gave us the all clear we all started looking for a place and coincidently five apartments had just become vacant nearby.

Emily and I decided to be roommates, Chloe and Nick obviously moved in together, and so did Hunter and Tori. Justin wanted a place to himself and Brey didn't oppose, so they each got their own places. Our office is in the Timmons building downtown on the eighth floor, suite A. As it turns out the organization we work for owns the building and the other three teams on our floor and very loose about the definition of classified.

Our office has three smaller offices and a room for meetings Brey and Nick share one, Tori and Justin share another, and we spies share the last. AG doesn't just pop up and more she tells us to go to the office then gives us our mission like a normal boss. The best part about all of these changes is the necessary shopping. When AG issued us our first pay check I was ecstatic after getting our apartment we had to get future and other house stuff. Then we needed to buy new clothes for the office and to fill up the empty space in my closet. Then I needed to buy a car and the dealer was very happy to help me out with that I ended up settling on a cute red convertible and Emily got a purple one. For the next two weeks or so we got used to our new normal then we got our next mission then they kept coming Jakarta, Auckland, Edinburgh, Wellington, Petra, Melbourne, Luxor, Manila, Lima, Santiago, Bogotá, Amsterdam.

Chapter 14

It has been four months, three weeks, two days, fourteen hours, and thirty-four minutes since Danny betrayed us, and it seems like I'm the only one who notices that he is gone. I sort of miss of having Danny around even though he hit me with a car and shot me in the shoulder.

Everyone else is so happy about the way things are now, but sometimes I like to drive up to the Villa and think about what it would be like if Danny was still here. I think he would like having more freedom, but he would make me pay for everything. From what I've heard Danny's in some underground prison probably going completely mad, and that's where he will stay until AG decides to kill him.

After we got back from Amsterdam I started driving up here because Danny and I always talked about going to Amsterdam and I don't like reminiscing at my place. When I arrived, I saw two trucks parked outside I knew AG would have another team moving in, but I didn't want it to be this soon or ever.

Since it would be weird sitting there watching the house I decided to go to a bar when I got a call from AG asking me to come to the office. AG usually only sends Nick or Brey on personal missions, so when I got to the office alone I was kind of nervous until Tori walked in looking just as nervous as me. We both sat in the meeting room then AG popped up on the monitor and started pouring out directions.

Basically, a new team was about to go on their first mission, and we aka me will monitor them and if absolutely necessary aid. Their first mission is to destroy a drug smuggling ring kind of like ours their ring is centralized in around one city. AG kept their names classified, but gave me their instead.

The three spies are KP, AL, and CJ, the three support techs are NV, EH, and TW, and the two assassins are JSR and JMR. An hour after they got off the plane Tori hacked into their surveillance and com systems then left the rest to me. Like normal I was the person watching everyone's back, but sadly they were just moving dots on a screen that I couldn't help make better choices.

First, they tried to find a dealer and become friends with them and gain their trust, and after that failed JMR had the idea to kill off as many other dealers as possible until there is trust. After JMR and JSR killed around thirty-seven people KP was able to finally gain their targets trust then they went silent for ten seventy-two hour periods.

While KP was under deep cover, JMR and JSR killed around twenty other people, and everyone else was making this cartel very uncomfortable by destroying everything they could. They were doing great until they blew up the wrong car and killed the dealer KP had spent most of mission getting close to. Forcing the rest of the group to question his involvement seeing as he always seems to live through these explosions, fires, and shootings.

They became even more suspicious when they tested him and he didn't do what they thought they would then somehow three days later he was in an underground cell getting the snot beat out of him. JMR and JSR were going to try to break him out but two police officers pulled them over an arrested them for a gun they had in the car which was illegal in the state they were in.

AL and CJ were trying to figure out what to do when a grenade came through the window leaving them in the hospital. NV and EH wanted to call for help, but TW didn't think anyone would show up. They really needed help, so I asked AG if this counted as absolutely necessary. She told me that I should've said when the first problem happened, and that it was necessary when the police arrested JMR and JSR. She told the rest of the team to be on standby, and told me to wait until they called for help.

After almost a week of them arguing EH and TW got in to a fight, and while the two were throwing blows and breaking stuff NV got on her comps. "This is A-216 requesting assistance," she said and repeated before I could plug in my mic. "This is A-214 explain the extent of your problem" I replied trying to buy time for everyone to get there stuff together, and get to the airport. She tried to tell me what went wrong, but her other two teammates wouldn't stop interrupting her. I told them that we would be there soon and that they should clean up the mess they made from there little scuffle. Then I called AG and she told everyone else, and thirty minutes later we were on a plane headed their way.

The second we got off the plane we went straight to work. Nick went to go get JSR and JMR which they said was easy with the badges they stole from the FBI awhile back. Emily and Hunter went to go get KP, and Haleigh went to the hospital to make sure whoever tried to kill them wouldn't come back. Brey, Tori, and I went to the hotel room where the rest of the team was hiding.

When we got into the room we walked in on two guys yelling at each other with a small girl in the middle trying to break it up. Brey threw one of them across the room and the other got scared and backed off. "So," I started "you said you needed help." The girl Nicole Vincent the poured out everything that went wrong again, and by the time that she was done Nick was on the way back with JSR and JMR.

After about thirty minutes Brey got really annoyed with the two guys who just wouldn't shut up. While Tori was trying to fix their computer which they just happened to destroy in their fight, and they wouldn't stop trying to tell her what to do. Brey kept asking if she could shoot them, and I kept telling her no until one of them pushed her and asked if she had a problem with him.

Then she kicked him in the chest knocking him through the window, and when he finally got the guts to walk back through the door. She knocked him back outside and locked the door behind him then looked at me and shrugged. When Nick finally got here with JMR and JSR and the second they walked in the room they both yelled "oh my god" and practically sprinted over to Brey to give her a hug.

Chapter 15

I can't believe that no one told me that Brey had sisters, and how could she keep this from us when we lived in the same house. The only person who did seem surprised was Nick, but he did meet Brey less than a month after her parents died. The fact is that I felt like we were actually close and she didn't even mention that she had a sister and she has two. After their long hug that obviously made Brey uncomfortable they said the normal stuff you say to someone that you haven't seen in a while.

How are you here, how have you been doing, and I've missed you so much. Brey smiled they didn't act like they haven't seen each other in years, but like seeing one of those family members that you only see around the holidays. She introduced them to us the both had mocha skin and dark brown hair, but Jazz has hazelnut eyes while Jackie has dark brown eyes. They both seem really nice and even offered to help me, but by the time they finished the sentence I had already fixed it.

When their communication systems were back on line I got to hear, someone screaming bloody murder on full volume. Hunter and Emily were in the process of rescuing Kenny Peirce when they got surrounded and now their pinned down wasting bullets. Hunter was pretty much dragging Kenny out of there while Emily was trying to keep the shooters at bay. After I hacked into their system I locked a few doors and direct them out of the building. After they were safely on their way back here I locked every entrance and exit of the building, and to make sure that they weren't followed Hunter had already cut the break lines of all the other cars he could find. Then they were about half a mile away the building exploded I don't know why, I don't know how but it did.

They took Kenny to the hospital and he was diagnosed with three broken ribs, a shattered jaw, a cracked eye socket, a total of twelve fractures in his arms and legs, and a concussion. All that meant was that he got beat up, probably with a bat, he's in a lot of pain, but he'll live. It had been three hours since we had gotten off the plane, and we've rescued one person, gotten two people released from police custody more or less legally, and repaired an infiltrative surveillance and communication system from bits and pieces.

I gave Terrance his computer back, and he gave me a hug and kissed me on the cheek. I kept thinking if Hunter was here this guy would A not get close enough to even touch me or B be unconscious on the floor. Nick was kind enough to say that I have a boyfriend rather than throwing him across the room.

Hunter was extremely protective of me and sometimes a bit jealous even though it can be annoying sometimes I know that it always comes from a really sweet place. Since we have been officially living together everything has been wonderful walks on the beach, dinner dates, and our wonderful time that we spend watching TV together.

We still spend enough time away from each other so that we don't go insane. Mine with Chloe and Brey while he has Nick and Justin. Lately he has been saying I love you even more often I enjoy it, but it's starting to weird me out. I asked Nick what was wrong and he said it was nothing, but Nick is a very terrible liar. So I knew he wasn't telling me something, but I knew he wouldn't say anything even if I put a gun to his head.

We got back home three days later and we went back to our regularly scheduled programing. They second we walked into our apartment I turned on the TV and laid on the couch. He walked over, gave me a kiss, and took the remote changing the channel. He sat down in the chair next to the couch and smiled. I went and sat on his lap making sure he couldn't see the TV, and gently tried to take the remote out of his hand.

He started kissing me running his fingers threw my hair and tossed the remote on the couch. Then he picked me up and started walking towards the bedroom. I jumped down, ran to the couch, and changed the channel back to what I was starting to watch. He laughed then sat down beside me. He wrapped his arms around me, and I felt so small, and warm, and loved.

A few hours later he asked if I was hungry and I Really could've gone for a pizza. He told me to put on something nice, made a phone call, and left. I called Chloe and Brey asking them to come over and took a shower as fast as possible. Hunter doesn't like going anywhere fancy so I was really freaking out about why we were going there.

The doorbell rang and I let Chloe, Brey, and Haleigh for some reason in. Haleigh went straight for my closet while Brey asked me what was going on, and I told her what hunter said. When Haleigh walked out of my closet she had three dresses that I forgot I even had, she forced me to try them on. The first two were way too much for much for my taste, but the third was perfect. It was a lavender one shoulder dress that came just below my knees with a bejeweled belt. Haleigh forced my hair in a bun and almost made me where heels until Chloe found a pair of silver flats.

After I was finished getting dressed the three of them left I sat there for about ten minutes trying to figure out what was going on. When Hunter walked through the door he was dressed in a suit and tie. He smiled at me and asked if I was ready to go, I nodded trying to keep it together. We went downstairs, got in the car, and went to this restaurant that was at the edge of a pier. We sat at a table in the back right next to these huge bay windows and watched the sun set as we ate. Everything was amazing like it was a dream after we ate dessert Hunter and I just sat there talking.

Then he took my hand and was somehow standing beside me starring me strait in my eyes. "Victoria Amber Jones you are the most Amazing, Smartest, Funniest, Honest, and Sweetest person that I have ever and probably will meet, and I don't know if this is Crazy, or Stupid, or if I'm a complete genius." He bent down to one knee and pulled a ring out of his pocket it was a large Amethyst surrounded by smaller diamonds. At this point I couldn't breathe, covering my mouth with excitement, and trying not to cry. Then said "Will you give me the ultimate honor of marrying you."

I really couldn't breathe I never thought that Hunter would ever want to get married and I was trying to think of any reason in the world for me not to say yes. I realized I couldn't I felt like he and all of his flaws were perfect for me, and I practically knocked him over kissing him. I stuck out my hand waiting for him to put the ring on my finger then he looked confused and asked if this was a yes. I nodded and he stood up finally giving me the ring and it was perfectly. After we left the restaurant we told everyone and everything was perfect for about twenty minutes. Then Istanbul, Singapore, Kiev, Shenzhen, Bucharest, Taipei, Brussels, Chennai, Marrakesh, Phuket, Edirne, Bali, Copenhagen, Agra, Varna, and Riyadh. That's not counting the times that AG sent either of us on some random super top secret stuff, so we didn't get to actually having a wedding for a while and we weren't really worried about it.

   Until we wiped a girl off the face on the earth it was like she had never existed no friends, no family, and then he sent her to the same place we sent Danny. Then I felt like it was time for Hunter and me to finally get married. Getting married means more to us than it does to most people.

   Normally it signifies that you want to share everything with that person and spend the rest of your life with them, but for us it also means that we accept that every person who would ever want to kill you will also try to kill me too. I didn't want to have a wedding or anything, but then Haleigh found a way to tell my sister and brothers. Now I have to plan a wedding while Haleigh and Emily were either trying to help or take control of everything. We ended up inviting around twenty people and had four people in the wedding my maid of honor and Sister Gabrielle and my brides maid Chloe, and Hunter picked Nick as his best man and Justin for his grooms man.

My dress was an ivory dress with a sweetheart neckline and bejeweled belt. It came just below my knees in the front and came to my ankles in the back. Our Emily and Haleigh appointed color scheme was lavender and white or grey depending on what mood they were in. Brey helped us with the paperwork, making sure everything was done correctly, and completed as quickly as possible even when she had to help certain people get things done faster.

Then there was the bachelor and bachelorette parties Nick and Justin sort of kidnapped Hunter at around ten and brought him back around noon the next day. While Brey, Chloe, and Gabby made me wiling get in to a car blindfolded then we drove for a while, and they made me go up some stairs I think. Then they finally took of the blindfold and I was a plane with the three of them plus Haleigh and about eight or nine male "dancers." Everything was awesome form what I remember since post tequila bottle number four is a fun looking blur. We came back from Mexico two days later three days before the wedding and so far, everything was perfect.

Chapter 16

I didn't think when AG told me to do it. I thought everything would go back to being the same afterwards, but it didn't. Now I'm watching two of my so-called friends getting married regretting saying yes to AG. To be fair she did tell me that nothing would be the same after, but I just that they wouldn't trust me for a while then I could try to rebuild that.

Then I was sent to twenty-five different countries and had to destroy a few more lives and in the mien time I've been living in LA. She said that she told them that I was I an extremely classified location, but she told Brey and Nick enough so they wouldn't killed me. When I blew up the safe house we were staying at I made sure there was enough time for them to get out, I shot Justin in a place that wasn't lethal, and I did nothing to Haleigh besides letting her see me smiling.

I really wanted to go down there just to mess with them, but I would've been shot on site. I felt like I needed to talk to someone and Justin wasn't an option since he was probably still pissed at me for shooting him. Nick has his thing with Chloe that I really don't want to mess with.

Leaving Brey who there is a fifty percent chance that she will kill me before I can say anything, but sadly she was my best shot. When I let myself in to her apartment I couldn't stop thinking that it was a bad idea. I sat down at the breakfast bar and waited for her to come in when I realized that she would try kill me. I grabbed a metal pan from the kitchen to try to block the knife that she was going to throw at me. When she walked through the door she shot me in the shoulder and I fell to the ground.

Then she walked over to and crouched down beside me and said that it would've been a good idea if I'd went to Justin. "So what are going to try to do" she said picking up the frying pan that I dropped. "Well, I thought that I could try to get your help convincing everyone else that I wasn't actually trying to kill them" I said. Then she laughed "well them you're going to need more than my help" she replied. "You could help me talk to Nick" I said trying to sit up.

"You could've just called and asked to talk to him" she said throwing a hand towel at me. I put it on my shoulder and stood up realizing there wasn't an exit wound and that this was going to hurt as Brey pulled out a pair of needle nose pliers and a bottle of rubbing alcohol. Ten minutes of trying not to scream too loudly, a lot of pain, and Brey calling me all sorts of names the bullet finally unleashed its self from my shoulder. She put a bandage on it and then told me to meet her and Nick at the Sandy Shores beachside poolside bar at around nine.

I didn't think about it that much but when I showed up Nick, Brey, and Justin where sitting at a table for four right next to the pool. When I walked over to the table Justin lost it while Nick asked Brey what was going on. "So Danny here paid me a visit to..." at that point Justin tackled me into the pool and we started to fight.

Brey and Nick where being of no help while my best friend was trying to drown me, and I was just trying to get him off of me. I got to the edge of the pool and pulled myself out while Justin was swimming to the edge. Brey tossed me a towel then told me to sit down, and when Justin managed to walk back to the table she asked "Are you done." He nodded very reluctantly then sat down snatching the towel that Brey was handing him. "So as I was saying" she started "Danny wants to explain what happened." "He shot me" he said threw gritted teeth, "and I shot him so stop bitching about it" she said getting annoyed.

"I had orders" I started "believe me I get that it wasn't the smartest thing I've done, and I'm sorry dude." He looked at Brey then Nick "So you two knew about this" he said.

"Yeah, don't lose sleep over it" Nick replied and Brey added that there is a lot of stuff that we didn't know. We sat there having a few more drinks and I thought it was a good idea for Justin and me to go to the beach for a little while.

The next morning I woke up on his couch with a really huge headache, and I couldn't remember exactly what happened, how that I got there, or what I had to drink that got me that wasted. I went to Dino's got us some breakfast since Justin was still asleep. I ended up eating mine with a girl who worked there.

She was absolutely gorgeous and we ended up talking until the end of her shift which was around three. When I left I ended up leaving a one hundred dollar tip and her gave me her number. Thankfully I'm still amazing when it comes to women, but I'm not "mr.one night stand" anymore it's more like dating a different girl every month. I've tried having a "relationship" with a few of them, and when that works out in any other way than pain and agony on both sides I might try it again. Until then I will wait till I find a girl that is Independent, smart, pretty, a badass, and won't try to kill me. The last one is the most important since it's usually the biggest problem.

I dropped of Justin's breakfast at around noon and he was talking about how easily I got drunk. He said that I lost my touch and that I just couldn't handle myself like I had in the past. I have always been able to do everything a bit better than Justin ever could especially when it comes to the alcoholic beverage department, so I decided that we were both going to go out to a few bars and whoever passes out first has to call and flirt with Brey.

Which isn't that bad but if the loser says anything stupid she will probably beat the hell out of them. That night we went out and after an astonishing twenty something drinks each Justin called and asked brey out to dinner and put it on speaker for all to hear. "Aye sho I wassh thinking at we shhood go out shometime" he said trying not to sound as drunk as he was. She laughed for about five minutes "No, and I know that this was a dare and I will destroy you and Danny later" she said then hung up.

We both laughed like there was a chance for both of us to be in one piece tomorrow and that was how completely wasted we were. We started talking to these two girls named Liz and Mary who were just as drunk as we were. Liz was pretty with gray eyes and red hair, and Mary was a pretty brunette with brown eyes. They ended up leaving with us Liz and Justin went in his room while Mary and I stayed on the couch. Then I remembered the reason I came to Myrtle Beach in the first place to fix a few things.

The next morning I woke up to the door slamming shut. I felt Mary laying on my chest, but something felt wrong. I moved my hand down her back when I felt something wet and warm, and I looked at my hand it was blood. I blotted up seeing the knife in her back and where it barely cut my stomach. I looked and checked Justin's room Liz's body was right beside the bed and she had a huge gash across her stomach. Then there was Justin laying on the bed that was soaked with blood he had a pillow over his face that was also covered in blood. At that point I started freaking out I ran out the apartment in just my pants and a hoodie I grabbed running out the door.

I got to the bottom of the stairs when I heard someone yell my name, but that didn't stop me from jumping in my car and speeding away as fast as possible. I had gotten a few miles away when this motorcycle pulled up next to me, and pointed a gun at me. I started to speed up then I turned right on to a one-way street cutting off two lanes of traffic. Then I started going even faster when I saw them in the rear view gaining on me, and I started weaving through traffic.

I turned onto this road that I knew was almost never used, so I could leave this unknown person who was trying to kill me in the dust. Then a navy blue truck came out of nowhere and rammed me off the road. This truck looked bad-ass it looked like it could pull a train or something else ridiculous, but that's all I could tell from what little I saw of it as it drove to my capsized car before I passed out.

Chapter 17

I woke up in a very dark and damp room, my head was spinning, and I was hanging on a rope dangling from the ceiling. Then Brey walked in holding a bat and her knives in a rolled up cloth case. She sat her knives on a nearby box, and looked at me like she wanted wipe me off the planet.

"So" she started "was killing Justin the only reason you came here." "What" I said in disbelief that she would think I would do something like that then she threw a knife into my left thigh about four inches above the knee. "WHAT THE FUCK" I screamed, she threw one in the same place in my right and two more above them heading towards my crouch area. I felt like both of my legs were on fire I wanted to scream, but I was scared she would throw another knife.

"Did you come here to kill Justin" she asked walking towards me with her bat in hand. I wish I just said that I didn't kill him, but I said "It's not what you think." She hit me in the stomach and knocked the wind out of me, and swung two more times before she started talking again. "Oh really, cause Nick saw you running out of his place and found the bodies" she said matter of factly.

She hit me two more times and I was pretty sure a few of my ribs were broken "I didn't kill them" I yelled before she stopped to stretch her arms. "Okay them so it was one of those girls" she replied. I told her that they were just two girls we met earlier that night. She hit me again when Nick walked in and said one word cops. The three of us have a certain distaste of the police since they always seem to mess things up or get in the way.

Brey got this spray and cleaned off her bat while Nick pulled the knives out of out of my legs. When he got to the last one he twisted it and said if I said anything that he would not only kill me, but he would make sure that I'd be in extreme pain the entire time I'd be dying. She cleaned off her knives and put them in their case hiding them in a compartment in the floor. Then a swat team burst through the door.

They took me to the hospital where they patched up my leg and gave me some morphine for my three broken ribs. Apparently I started talking about Justin, Mary, and Liz while I was asleep. They arrested me and sat me in a gray interrogation room for a few hours until this guy walked in.

He was around five one in his early fifties, he had greyish brown hair and piercing green eyes.

"So Mr. Lawson" he started "do you know what those two people wanted" he asked acting like he didn't care. I answered no then he asked if I knew who they are. I said no again and he just nodded his head before asking if I knew a Maryann Hughes. I again said no then he stood up and glared at me "so tell me why we found your DNA in her body." "Well when a man and a woman love each other very much" I started before he shot me a look that forced me to shut up. "So you two slept together" he asked I said yes, and asked other questions concerning how we met and what happened that night and I left in the details.

Then he left the room and this female officer walked in saying that she was here to take my finger prints. She was sort of plain dark brown hair, brown eyes, and in her early thirties. When she took my hand I stood up watching her amazement when she realized I didn't have any. She tried my left hand I wrapped my arms around her a asked her questions like how long she had been working here, her name, what school did she go to, if she liked it, and what else she liked.

She eventually asked me to back up and I asked her if she would put me in handcuffs if I didn't then I backed up. "So, were you born yesterday or something" she asked. I told her no then asked if she had ever found a blank slate before me.

She said none before today sounding disappointed. "Well can I go, or do I need to sit here for the next two days" I asked. She said no of course and that I shouldn't act like this was a game. "But it's funny that they've arrested the only people who wouldn't kill J and believe me it's a long list" I said. She asked why any I told her that he wasn't the safest person in the world and she said that I wasn't either. Then the guy detective walked back in, whispered something in her ear. And then she left. A few minutes later she walked back in Brey in handcuffs then they both left.

I don't think they knew what they were trying to achieve but that wasn't going to happen. We both stood there silently and very awkwardly until the guy officer walked back in and started to ask us both why she had been beating me up. I said I don't know and Brey just gave him a blank stare, and that just pissed him off. He started yelling at the both of us about how we were both going to jail for the rest of our lives if we didn't tell him something.

I said I don't know anything and Brey continued her blank stare. Then he grabbed Brey by her arm and took her out of the room. Then the female officer walked back in and asked me if I wanted to go to prison. I told her no, and then she asked why I wouldn't say anything. I don't know why but I told her that it was a bit above her paygrade, but then she looked hurt and I started feeling bad.

Then the guy officer walked back in pushing nick in there with me and after seeing me. He looked at the guy and asked him if he thought this would really work. After another round of him yelling he pulled Brey back in then started a new approach. "One of you in here ratted the other two out" he started "so it's best for all of you to come clean." Brey continued her blank stare while Nick and I both just laughed. "Well if you don't believe me ask her" he said pointing a Brey, and then Nick laughed even harder.

"What, y'all are so close that you don't think she would open her mouth" he said mockingly. Nick just took off his handcuffs and said that they had absolutely nothing. Then he tried to leave the room and was easily stopped. Then there was a knock at the door and both the guy and girl officer left. About twenty minutes later the very grumpy officer came back in and said "you're free to go" Brey took off her handcuffs and the three of us started walking out then he said not you two grabbing Brey's arm. She started cussing him out in sign language and he had the 'oh fuck' face for a full five minutes. Afterwards I said that I wasn't pressing charges pulling Brey out of his grasp and putting my arm around her giving her a little kiss on the cheek.

He was about to give us our stuff when the female officer or detective Mooney asked us to look at a video. It was the video camera in Justin's apartment that was facing the door we watched the four of us walking in to the apartment at that point Brey pushed my arm off her shoulder.

Then another person walked in she had black hair, hazel eyes, and olive skin, and eight and a half minutes later she ran out. Then another four minutes and thirty seven seconds later I was sprinting out, and Nick walked in a minute later. I defiantly recognized and I think Nick and Brey did too it was Rebecca Cairn an ex-spy and one of Justin's ex-one night stands.

We told them that we had no clue who she was and then the guy officer or detective Harmon finally let us leave. Brey got her truck and Nick's bike from the impound yard then we left. She took me back to my hotel and I asked her if she would like to come up. Then she punched me in the face so hard that I was surprised that I stayed conscious. The next morning the both of them called me and asked if I wanted to go on a little road trip and hang out with Rebecca. I said yes of course was kind of set on a little revenge.

CHAPTER 18

I felt like I had been in the car for an eternity. I don't know whose idea it was to drive from South Carolina all the way to Atlantic City, but I think they got the idea that this was a bad on at about four am. The thing I hated most of all is that I wasn't the one driving. Here I am the best freaking driver in the world and I'm sitting in the back seat.

The good part is that Brey was sitting there with me, but most of the time she was asleep. I always thought she was pretty and it looks like while I was away she got a lot hotter. Now I had to focus on not staring at her, and I have to tell myself that she will kill me if she caught me starring at her like this. Then I started think about what would happen if we did go out and whether she would really kill me. Then I realized she was laying on my shoulder and I don't know what possessed me to do this but I wrapped my arm around her shoulder and laid my head against hers. It felt nice and

I ended up falling asleep, but I woke up when she pushed me up against the window.

It was around seven pm when we finally arrived and finished checking into our hotel. I got bored in my room and I guess Brey was too since she invited me to the bar with her. When I got to the hotels bar I was her sitting in the corner drinking what looked like whiskey or something.

I walked over to her, sat in the chair across from her, and looked at the glass she had poured for me. "So, what are we drinking to" I asked. "The life and unexpected demise of Justin Anderson, who would have thought any of us would get to die in our sleep" she replied. "What, are you practicing your eulogy" I said sarcastically. She smiled "so how fucked up are you feeling" she asked taking a sip of her drinking. "Very" I said gulping back my entire glass, and whatever she had picked to drink was stronger than I expected. "Sorry I forgot you weren't a whiskey person" she said finishing her glass.

She smiled at me when I poured the both of us another glass and then I asked her why she didn't seem so broken up. "I don't cry when someone gets to go to heaven" she replied. I didn't think she was religious in any way, but I guess her believing in an afterlife or God isn't too weird since I do. Now that I think about it most killers believe in heaven and hell or something similar.

I tossed backed a few more drinks trying to stop thinking about how my best friend and I will never get out and get completely drunk again, how I won't get to have him be my wingman to pick up extremely intoxicated girls, and how I will never beat him in mortal combat again. Then I thought about how much I wanted to kill Rebecca for killing my best friend and those two girls.

I was finally able to turn off the fillings of hatred and depression when I thought about how of all people who knew Justin Brey knew that I would need revenge and strong liquor. After an hour or so I went to my room, and went straight to sleep think about Brey. Then I realized that was the second time I fell asleep thinking about her and that she had broken the record of how many times I had thought about being with a girl.

The next morning nick called me at nine am which would've been fine if I didn't have a small hangover. We ended up going to a penthouse suite in another hotel where the three of us were patted down upon arrival. After Brey and Nick handed over all of their guns and knives they both talked to this woman for a while. She had dark brown hair, brown eyes, chocolate skin, and a warm smile. "You can come over here Daniel I don't bite" she said. I walked over and sat down next to Brey and I was nervous for some reason. "Zamora, can you get my laptop from the back room please" the woman said, and Brey said yes ma'am then walked out of the room. Then she leaned closer to me, batted her eye lashes, and asked "So, Daniel how long have you been eyeing my Granddaughter."

Nick looked at me like I was crazy for a few seconds then asked to be excused and she told him that he "most certainly could not." "Um, not for very long ma'am" I said hoping that it was the right answer. She smiled then Brey walked back in the room handing her grandmother the laptop. "Honey, since you're up can you get us something to drink, Nicky will help you" she said with a smile, then they went into another room. She scooted even closer to me almost on my lap, then she had a straight razor at my neck. "Now Daniel if you so much as think of hurting my dear, sweet, Zamora I will come out or retirement and invent a whole new way of torturing and killing a person just for you, you understand" she said mincingly. I nodded in agreement or out of pure fear. Then she put the razor away then gave me a hug returning to her sweet and kind persona. Then Brey and Nick walked back in with a few glasses of sweet tea.

"So, from what I understand you are here to track down a pesky little girl" Brey's grandmother or Mrs. Kathy as Nick called her, said. The three of us answered "yes ma'am" at the same time. "So, how are you going to kill her" she asked with excitement. "Grandma" Brey objected. "Oh hush up, I just want to know" she said. Nick looked like he would rather be anywhere else in the world. Then she gave him a stern look, and he said that he didn't care as long as she dies and I agreed with him. Then we were told how we were no fun and that we needed to live a little while we were young. After she forced us to have brunch with her, she told Brey that she could use her torture room if she needed. Then she told us to check with the front desk for Ms. Cairn's home address, and that is was nice seeing us.

We went down to the front desk and Brey talked to the concierge. He acted snotty to us when we tried to ask nicely. Then Brey jumped over the counter and put a knife at his neck. Then he not only gave us her address but the credit card number they had, a copy of her driver's licenses, and a cell phone number. We went to the address that she gave the concierge which was only an few hours away. We pull up to this plain house in the middle of this neighborhood, and every house looked almost identical to each other. We found her house in the sea of copies and the only differences were the last name Clark on the mail box and one car in the driveway that was obviously made for two.

We made sure that no one was in the house, then picked the lock, and went inside. Everything looked neat and put up, but still lived in and homely. We looked around and found a lot of pictures of her and some guy and she looked happy in them. Then we found a huge wedding photo in the formal dining room. Then I went down stairs and put a small explosive next to the gas heater. Then we went outside and waited for her to return. There Nick said what all of us were thinking "why would she kill Justin an ex if she moved on already." We knew all knew what we were going to do, so when she and her husband pulled up and started walking to the door. I pressed the button turning their house into an enormous ball of flames. The both of them looked horrified, frozen, starring at the inferno that was their home. Brey called the fire department, and we went to our hotel for the rest of the night.

The next day they checked in to the hotel that Ms. Kathy lived at. We waited an hour, then just took the all access key we got from the concierge, and walked right in. Her husband tried to put up a fight that lasted a whole two seconds before Nick knocked him out. Then Rebecca tried to attack Brey, and after Brey broke her arm and probably a few ribs she passed out on the floor. We dragged them down to the basement and tied them to some chairs then we waited for them to wake up behind a wall of shelves. Her husband woke up first and instantly started screaming for help and trying to escape. Which woke up Rebecca who after a failed attempt to calm him down told Greg, which was his name, to shut up and that made him start panicking. They started confessing their love for each other. Brey got bored and annoyed with the both of them and she walked in and punched her in the face.

"I'm not telling you anything" Rebecca snarled. "Well, I guess you can go then" Brey responded sarcastically as she took a bottle of lighter fluid and a book of matches off the shelf. "Please let us go" Greg pleaded as she drenched him in the lighter fluid. She just laughed at him then said "no, I'm gonna kill your wife here, but whether or not you die to is up to her." "So, Becca" Brey started "you killed some people a few days ago and I want to know why." "I said I'm not" and before she could finish her sentence Brey struck a match and tossed it at Greg. It missed his body causing him scream a little "Now, if you don't your hubby here will be barbeque" she said. "I-I-I'm not" Rebecca stuttered, Brey tossed another match making them both scream. "I was only there to kill the Guy, Justin, the other three were just there and I panicked" Rebecca said as fast as she could.

"Why did you kill him," Brey asked in her daunting apathetic voice. Rebecca looked at Brey like she hated and was terrified of her. Then she looked at her scared and confused husband as Brey held a lit match over his head, and Brey said "any day now." Looking at her husband again he mouthed the word please, and the Rebecca broke into tears "it was a hit, they said if I killed him I could finally be out of this life" she sobbed.

Brey put out the match, creeped closer to her, and with a sinister look asked "Who are they." Rebecca responded with "I swear on my life I don't know then turned into a blubbering mess crying, saying sorry to her husband, and begging Brey not to kill him. Nick and I walked from behind the wall of shelves, and the second she saw me she started crying even harder. "They're going to kill us" she sobbed over and over. I don't know why, but I bent down beside her, wiped away some of her tears, and said "don't worry I'll kill you."

Nick and Brey poured another bottle of lighter fluid on Greg, and then gagged him. Rebecca begged me to save him, but I reminded her of the two girls she killed who did nothing to her. Brey struck a match and tossed it into the lap of the poor guy, and I almost felt sorry for the guy. Then I looked at the cold, emotionless faces of Brey and Nick, and they almost seemed sad as well to see a guy who still doesn't know why he is dying be turned into a big ball of flames.

After Rebecca gave up on trying to save him Brey shot him to put him out of his misery while Nick extinguished the corpse. "YOU'LL BURN IN HELL FOR THIS" Rebecca screamed at the three of us before bursting into tears. Thinking about it two assassins nicknamed after the Greek gods of Panic and Fear, and me a guy who is known for blowing up buildings and cars while killing hundreds of people.

If this was the deciding factor we had a very late decision. Brey knocked her out, then we tied her up and wrapped her up in plastic wrap till she looked like a mummy with only her eyes and nose exposed. We put her in the trunk then drove an hour away to the place we all agreed was where she would die, a nice little lake. We rented a boat, rode to the center of the lake, tied some cement blocks around her, woke her up, and threw her over the edge. I sat there watching her sink till she was just a trail of bubble leading to the surface.

Nick had brought a cooler with us since we had to rent the boat for the hour, and we might as well celebrate the death of Justin's killer. I don't know how but somehow between beer number five and six I was talked into a game of truth or dare. I didn't take a dare because I didn't want to do something crazy or stupid, so I had to answer a lot of very uncomfortable questions.

The both of them asked questions like, where was I for the past few years, what was I doing, how many girls had I slept with, and how many people have I killed all normal questions. Except for one question Brey asked that I didn't want to answer "Out of the Tori, Chloe, Haleigh, Emily, and I who would you date and why?" Then I said I changed my mind to dare, and Nick's dare was to answer the question. I finished beer number eight and answered truthfully "You" pointing at Brey, and she asked why.

I answered I don't know and she told me to guess, so I thought of some reasons "you're super smart, fun to hang out with, very determined, independent, and extremely hot." Nick asked if I had thought about this before, and I said that Justin and I talked about it a lot. Then it was Brey's turn and nick dared her to jump in the lake or admit that he was a better shot than her. By the time Brey got back in the boat our hour was up, and we returned the boat then went to a hotel for the rest of the night.

The next morning AG sent us a message about Justin's funeral and as it turns out he is having two. One for the eight of us and his sisters and brother who live here, and another in the UK for the rest of his family. His funeral was the weirdest felling ever and everything just felt too real. His two sisters spoke about their favorite memory of him and how happy, funny, and lively he was. The funniest thing was that his brother talked about him like they were best friends, but Justin said that the guy was annoying and didn't like being around him.

I felt like I was the only one who really knew him even over his own family and started thinking about the one actual promise we made to each other. That day when we both planned to do something stupid at each other's funeral, and I decided to keep my word. I sat in the back and plotted exactly when I was going to do this then I connected my phone to the speakers and played the unedited version of one of Justin's favorite songs my last by Big Sean. His brother was furious, but it seemed to make everyone else smile.

After leaving the funeral I couldn't get the song out of my head. For the entire drive home Brey was asleep and I just sitting there looking at her laying her head against the window, eyes closed, with the sun making her chocolate skin look a goldish color. Nick told me that I looked creepy and that she knows I'm in to her.

I asked him if he told her and he told me that she wasn't an idiot. I didn't even realize that I was being that obvious, and I got an idea that would either be my best idea ever or get me killed. After we got back to her apartment the three of us were chilling on her balcony and Nick went inside for to get a drink or something. Then I took her hand pulled her close to me and kissed her.

CHAPTER 19

Once I thought my life would be boring, then I fell in love with Nick and that flew out of the window. Now I have to focus on looking normal for him even though he never asked me to lie for him it became second nature. He said it was the spy in me taking over trying to keep everything from getting too crazy.

Other than my bouts of compulsive lying I have a pretty normal day to day life. I work for Burnett reality group as one of their fifteen agents and I specialize in condos and starter homes which I'm very good at. I have a few friends like Josh, Amber, Katie, and Denis.

Josh is a really exuberant person, fun to hang out with, and extremely nosey he is about six one, brown eyes, and tan skin. Amber always has gossip about everyone else and is also suspiciously interested in Nick, but I love this five one, brown skinned, plump woman. Katie thinks I need to dump Nick since she things he is gone too much for her likening, and she thinks he is hiding something, yet whenever this five four, thin, red headed sees him she acts like they are great friends. Then there is Denis who absolutely hates Nick even though Nick hasn't said two words to the guy, and other than that he is really nice to me. He has blond hair, grey eyes, is about five eleven, and tan skin.

I really like all of the people at my job except that bitch Sabrina, She thinks I lie about everything and even thinks that Nick is made up and that I hire an actor to not look as sad. I want to punch her in the face and I swear one day I will snap and tell her about herself.

Whenever Nick isn't working he brings me lunch or we go out together just too spent time with each other, and Sabrina always tries to come with us and Nick says that he just wants to spend some time with me., thankfully that usually makes her back off. Even when Nick likes to surprise me the moment he gets back from somewhere and the receptionist Harper always lets him in then tells everyone but me.

My boss Mr. Burnett or Terry as he likes to be called is really sweet, nice, and a really giving person each month we have to do some charity event and he counts it as a team building exercise. I have asked Nick if he would want join in with and each and every time he says no and that kind of makes Terry a little upset who is very determined about it.

Two weeks after we got back from Justin's funeral I was in a meeting and the topic came up of our team building exercise for the month. This month we were going to have a little outing and Terry insisted on me asking Nick to join us, but Nick had left on a mission three days ago.

I tried to explain that he was on a business trip but Sabrina insisted that I call him and got Terry behind her, and now with me being the center of attention I called him and put it on speaker. The second he answered the first thing we heard was gunfire. "Hey what's up" he said sounding very calmly. "Nothing much I just wanted to ask you something" I replied, "Is it important" he asked. "Kind of, but I can call back later" I said. "No your fine, these guys can't shoot for shit anyways" he replied playfully. "Um okay, at work we are all going out, and I was wondering if you would like to join in with us" I asked. "Baby" he sighed reluctantly.

"Please I really want you to do this with me" I said. "Okay how mad would you be if I said no" he asked. I said very then there were few very loud gunshots and everything got quiet. "I don't know if I am going to be able to make it" he said and after I reminded him that he doesn't know when it is he asked if he really had a choice and I told him no. "Fine, but Rena has to come to" he said. I said okay after terry gave me a reassuring nod then he said that that he needed to go and that he would be back in two days.

After I hung up Dennis asked what Nick did for a living and I said the only profession that was still fit but wasn't actually true and said that he was a Defense Contractor and that his organization operates under the government.

After Nick got back he picked me up for lunch, and everyone seemed to try to avoid him except for Sabrina of course. I was almost done closing a sale when Terry got up the courage to ask him in to his office, and I have to say that was the fastest talk terry has ever had with someone.

I felt him behind my chair and when he put his hands on my shoulders the entire room around us tensed up a little. Then he asked in a whisper "why is everyone looking at me like I going to kill them?" "Well I told them that you're a mercenary," I whispered back. He wrapped his arms around my neck and watched the eyes fill with a bit of fear, and all he did was smile. He kissed me on the cheek and the we went to lunch leaving everyone a little more terrified then when they came in. While at lunch he and I talked about everyone's reaction and then he tried to get out of going shooting but that still didn't happen.

After I got back from lunch Katie, Amber, and Josh asked to come over, which was perfectly fine since he was going to work out with Brey. Josh brought the pizza and Amber brought the wine and the three of us were just chilling in the living room. The way our apartment is set up there is the kitchen which opens into the living room and we have a small eating area in between them.

To the right is our bedroom where we had our own bathroom, the guest bathroom, and the guest bedroom which somehow turned into Nick's gun room. That obviously has a lock on the door that only Nick and I know the passcode to since Nick did something that makes it almost impossible to break into. Josh mistook it for the bathroom once and was almost electrocuted.

When Katie finally arrived, we watched some tv and chilled out until Nick got back from the gym then it felt like Katie had started her own intervention. "I'm sorry but I thought you would be with a sweet guy" she said. "well he is really sweet" I replied. "yeah, I was thinking more like flowers just because, romantic, high effort kind of sweet" she replied. "well I'm not into that I like perfect gentleman, overprotective, realistic kind of sweet" I replied. Then Nick fresh out the shower walked in the living room "so you ready to go shooting tomorrow" amber asked. He shot her an annoyed look and said that he wasn't looking forward to it.

When she asked why he said that he didn't want to make us look bad, and an intoxicated Katie took it as a challenge. "shoo you think you so great at eve er re thing you're not that cool I bet that you will lose" she said barely able to sit up. Nick laughed then took her keys off the counter and put them in one of the drawers "really" he said. Amber tried to change the subject but Katie was out for blood "Fight me right now" she said trying to stand.

She kicked off her shoes and started to tie back her hair Nick stared at her like she was joking, but sadly she wasn't. He walked from behind the counter over to her trying to just hug it out then she swung at him, He dodged it of course but it came close. Then he grabbed her arm and pined it behind it her and sat her on the couch she sat there a bit too drunk to stand un till she fell asleep. Josh, amber and I thought it was funny. An hour or so later Josh the only sober one drove Katie and Amber home and Nick and I went straight to sleep.

The next day we were going to the range which was thirty minutes away from our apartment and since Nick didn't try to back out of going we got there earlier that the rest of the group. Nick got impatient and decided to go inside and a few minutes later I went in to check on him.

After I walked in this tall man with coffee colored skin said, "so you must be Chloe" then gave me a hug. "Nice to meet you" I replied giving Nick a confused look who thought this was weird was looking at the guy like he was about to hit him. When he let me go he told me that he was glad to put a face to the name then walked back behind the counter. Nick wrapped his arm around my shoulder and told me that the man's name was Darrell and that he owns the shooting range.

"I could get you guys set up outside are you doing long or short range today" he asked. Nick told him that he was with the group and Darrel said that he was trying to show off Nick just shrugged it off. Thankfully Mr. Barnette walk in and took Darrell's attention he made us all fill out some paperwork and by the time everyone got there and we were ready to go it was ten o'clock.

This wasn't my first time shooting, my dad took me all the time, but this was the first time Nick has seen me shoot and everything I shot was in a small cluster just left of the target. The entire time I was shooting Nick was just sitting behind me then Denis asked him if he was going to shoot any then Brey walked in. she asked him if he was ready.

They walked over to the last two targets, gave each other a nod, then they snatched their guns from their waistbands and started shooting. Everyone crowed around them and they were so focused like it was just the target. Their guns went off like they were automatics changing magazines in just seconds with casings flying in a constant string next to them. When they were done their targets looked almost identical with the head and chest blown out. Mr. Barnette asked me to remind him to never piss him off. Sabrina had been quiet for the entire time until she saw Brey then she opened her mouth and asked who Brey was.

I told her that she was Nick's friend and then she asked how close are they and if they hung out a lot. Then Nick walked back over to me and she just stared at him and out of the corner of my eye saw her start talking to Brey who was holding a AR-15. Then handed me his gun and placed his arms on top of mine a few shots later I was hitting the center of the target. Then the let go and I was still hitting the center. I heard Brey say "you need to take the butt of the gun off your shoulder" then a loud shot and Sabrina scream.

Darrell took her in the back and Brey stood there trying not to laugh. We were pretty much done after that and went to get some lunch. The Nick got a call, said some stuff in Russian then told me he had to leave. A few days later I was at work and I heard harper screaming at someone then she suddenly stopped. When I turned around I saw Chase pointing a gun at Denis who had wedged himself between us.

He told him to move, and Denis told him that he would have to go threw him then he shot him in the shoulder. I ran for the door and the second I opened it Danny was standing there he gave me a wink, pushed me into the wall, and injected me in the neck with something.

I woke up laying in a bed that was in a light purple room with pictures lining the walls most of which were of Chase his wife and their daughter Olivia. I looked out the room and saw it was snowing, like real snow, not the ground up ice they had at almost every winter festival back home. The strange thing was that it was the middle of March the last time I checked.

I sat up and was met with a wave of dizziness and when I was finally able to stand I started to walk around the house and since there was no one in the other two bedrooms down stairs, kitchen, living room, or dining room I checked upstairs and found no one in the two bedrooms or Tv/Olivia's playroom.

I heard what sounded like someone at the door and ran back downstairs into the room I woke up in. I heard chase walking towards the door and after getting myself together I opened it. "good morning girlie" he said smiling. I asked what was going on and he said, "Nick just got paranoid about something" like it was stupid for him to worry about me. I followed him to the kitchen and sat down at the table, and he gave me a glass of water then asked me if I was feeling okay.

Then Julia asked if I was hungry which I was then she heated up a plate that was in the fridge then asked if I was okay with staying there for a while. I answered yes then Olivia ran in giving me a hug almost knocking me over. She had gotten so big since I saw her last and that was Christmas.

I spent the next week chilling, playing with Liv, and relaxing with Abby. Nick called twice making sure I was okay and Danny popped in a few times. From what Danny 'didn't' tell me they were working for an extremely dangerous person and they were Rich enough to hire all of them even Chase.

When Nick walked in the first thing he did was kiss me, his lips were warm and soft I felt like I was melting from the waist down as he pulled me away I felt like the breath was being sucked out of me. then Liv practically tackled him he gave her a hug and I then I saw Danny and Brey hugging outside with Danny lifting her feet off the ground after they were done liv went in for her hug pushing Danny into the snow. We ate dinner and after Olivia went to sleep Nick and I retreated in to my room.

Inside he wrapped his arms around my waist and kissed me "I'm sorry about all of this" he said and I told him that it was okay. We kissed once or twice or a few times I felt my feet lift off the ground and next the cold sheets touching my skin. I felt how warm his chest and back was, then his cool and hair between my fingers and how wonderful the tingle up my spine felt.

When I woke up I was alone underneath the sheets and couldn't seem to find any of my clothes. When Nick walked in he was wearing a solid black dress shirt, jeans, and boots, and was carrying a suitcase and bag in one hand and a bathrobe in the other.

He handed me the bathrobe and tossed both bags on the bed. "So where are you going" I asked putting on the robe, and he sat on the bed and opened the bag. "can't tell me uh" I said with a sigh, he answered me by taking two guns that were already in there holsters out of his bag and strapping one to each side of his waist.

I and asked what was in the suitcase expecting that he wasn't going to give an answer, but he said that since we or I was going to be here for a while that I would need some more clothes. I asked how long a while was going to be and he told me that he didn't know then strapped a knife to the back of his waist band next putting a few magazines in his pocket.

Then he turned to me and asked how he looked. I told him that he looked nice and that he needed a jacket. I gave him a kiss and he kissed me back I sort of melted again I started at the knot of my robe and he took my hand and put something in it and pulled away and said, "God I love you." Without skipping a beat, I said I love you too. Then he asked, "do you mind wearing that for me" pointing at my hand, and after looking at the diamond ring that was in my hand I said yes and kissed him. Then I asked if this was for real and he said that it was if I wanted it to be. I kissed him again then he said that if anyone asks we have been engaged for about a month or longer.

I agreed to his terms and then there was a knock at the door. Brey, Chase, and Danny they were dressed like Nick with slight differences. Brey's jacket came to her mid-thigh and was wearing lace up ankle boot that had a three-inch heel, Danny was carrying a bag, and Chase was wearing dress pants. "Let's go we're already running late" Chase said tossing Nick a jacket I kissed him again and the four of them walked out.

Two days later Abby got a call from Chase and kept shooting me a worried look then she wrote down some stuff, hung up and made another call. I didn't get off the couch until I heard her say my address then she handed me the phone and told me to give them the pass code to Nicks gun room.

I was scared that this was a test put she had this look like it was a life or death type of thing, so I told them the code "zero-four-two-three-zero-seven-one-nine" the voice said thank you and that the package will be there in thirty-six ours. Then Julia took the phone back and mouthed the words thank you and told them Brey's address and said that there wasn't anything to worry about then hung up. I asked her that was going on and she told me not to worry and that we were all moving.

The next thing I knew I was helping her pack her and Olivia's stuff up then I was in the car being taken to god knows where for a reason that Abby didn't know. When we stopped for gas I asked her where we were going and she told me that chase had bought a house in Tennessee and that where we were moving there. The house was in the middle of nowhere surrounded by woods at the top of a mountain with a road that was barely big enough for one car.

Once we got up there I realized that the house was a lot bigger that we thought there were a total of eight bed rooms spread across the three levels of the home and everything was already fully furnished. One in the basement which looked like a mancave with a bedroom and bathroom. The ground floor was home to a guest bedroom and bathroom on one side, the kitchen, dining, and living room, then three more bedrooms that shared two bathrooms.

The second level had two bedrooms that shared a bathroom and the master bedroom and bathroom. These were all things that were at their old house then there was the rest of the property. Behind the house was a nice outdoor living area with a pool and a ten-car garage, and there was a treehouse that Olivia seemed really excited about.

Half a mile away from the house there was a helicopter, landing pad, and two strangely large sheds. I went inside one and it was very creepy and was giving me torture room vibes with blood stains on the floor and chains hanging from the rafters. When I got back to the main house I realized that you couldn't even see that it existed through the trees and distance.

The next morning, we woke up to someone at the door after Julia answered it, and string of guys carrying boxes came in. Abby directing them where to put everything by what address it came from all the stuff from Nick and I's apartment went into one of the rooms down stairs, the stuff from Brey's apartment into another, and some stuff from some place in North Dakota in another I guess that was Danny's stuff but I wasn't sure.

Then they asked where to put these big cases they had that were obviously filled with all the weapons, and she directed them to the sheds, showed them the dirt road that lead down there, and they put everything in the not creepy shed. Then we spent the next three days unpacking everything and Olivia was even nice enough to help us in reward for pizza which sound great for me.

Everything was so far away I almost wished I could fly the helicopter. After we took thirty minutes driving to the closest grocery store and two hours of shopping then another drive back we were greeted by Chase, Danny, Brey, and Nick. Then things seemed a little more normal Nick was home with me at least twice a week and I felt like I wasn't all alone when he was gone.

When I finally got another phone I told Katie, Josh, Denis, and Amber that I was fine and that I was engaged then they told me how Sabrina was saying that I was dead and how Nick killed me. After I talked to them Denis just stopped talking to me and the rest of them I guess I read that wrong but since then everything has been great.

Epilogue

There is this roller coaster in Tideland that after you get strapped in and go about a hundred feet in the air you come to the end of the track and you stop. Then the very tack that you are on rotates a full one hundred eighty degrees and connects to the rest of the track at a huge drop straight down, and after it lets you stare at the distance between you and the ground before you drop.

That what it was like, first knowing that something was wrong, then everything changing, Then the drop. AG gave us our mission a month after Justin's funeral and since we were still pretty broken up about it and it just felt wrong without him. She gave us an easy one all we had to do is to take Aijhia Miller, the daughter of Geovanni Miller who is the leader of a very dangerous organization, from a holding cell in Las Vegas to a secret prison. While trying to get her to say anything about what her father can do or how far his reach goes.

When we went to pick her up she had found some way to get a phone call to an untraceable number we told Ag about it and she said that she was going to send her to a different location which turned out being the Regale building. Then we put a bag over her head and got her in the car after she tried to escape a few times we got on the road with her sitting between Haleigh and I in one car, hunter driving another with Tori and Max and Aaron in another.

Went in the same direction for the entire drive following close behind each other. Then max and Aaron's car swerved and went into a ditch. Next these two people on motorcycles started driving next to us they pulled up to the driver and passenger seat then Shot them both. Making us almost crash thankfully Haleigh was able to steer us into a ditch, but they came back around with their guns trained on the car.

They stopped at the edge of the ditch and got off their bikes and I heard a helicopter in the distance. I was so glad about it thinking that AG had a chopper following us like she had done in the past it reassured my just knowing that all I had to do was hold them off.

They were on either side of the car I gave Haleigh a nod and we opened the door and lunged at them. They obviously dodged the car door, but the first thing I grabbed was their gun and threw it to the ground. Then played with the blind spots in their helmet getting a few punches in their gut, but they didn't seem to be phased by a single one of them.

Then they proceeded to kick my ass starting with punches in the face, stomach and a kick to the chest sending me the ground. The I grabbed handful of sand and threw it in their face then kicked the temporarily blinded helmet sending them on back a few steps. Then they took off his helmet revealing Nick's sarcastic face "I was being nice" he said. "well don't be" I snarled back. "Fine" he said with a shrug then a few seconds later I was face down in the sand with blood running from my nose and lip. I rolled over to see the helicopter land and the three of them climb inside then fly off.

Then Hunter and Tori pulled up with Aaron and Max already inside. The next thing I knew I was in AG's office with her starring me down. "what happened again" she said like she didn't believe us or didn't believe any of it. Hunter was done with it "GOD DAM IT WE'VE BEEN OVER THIS" he shouted. "We have got an agent in the hospital, a criminal on the loose, and your saying that the second and third best assassins in the western hemisphere are working for the most dangerous man in North America right now" She spat back.

"I'm sorry if I am double checking" she said. Then AG's assistant walked in holding a stack of files, and the first think Max asked was if there was any news on Haleigh. She was still unconscious, but has become the only person in the world to get in the way of anyone in the Rena family and live. Then her assistant handed her the three files in her arms then left as fast as possible, and AG read the names on the files then looked at us. First, she drank the rest of her tea then took her mug and filled it with Whisky taking a big swig or two.

She sat back down at her desk and reread the front cover of the files then drank a few more sips. "What is it now" Hunter said. "It seems that their contracts were not renewed at their demand" she said. "WHAT THE HELL DOES THAT MEAN" Hunter yelled. Tori took him by the wrist forcing him to sit down while AG finished her whiskey. "What does that mean" Tori asked nicely. "That means that we aren't in charge of or in control of the three of them" She answered. "The three of them?" Tori asked.

"Yes, Brey, Nick, and Daniel" she said starring at the files. "Here is what is going to happen, first you are going to try to convince Brey, Nick, and Daniel not to blow your covers, then you are going to infiltrate Mr. Miller's organization and destroy it, and after all of this is over you will be transferred to the CIA" she said. I asked her why would we be transferred and she simply said that our contracts were up and that it was time for us to move on. I left her office with an eerie feeling like this was not going to end well, but we knew exactly what we had to do.

We got back to Myrtle Beach and went to the place where Chloe worked, but the people there said that she was kidnapped three weeks ago. This one woman Sabrina pointed out everyone who was really close to her, and we talked to them turns out they talked to her via a video call but they didn't know where she was.

We called her back and tried to track it, but Tori ran into her own fire wall that she was kind enough to make so strong the she couldn't get through it. Thankfully Chloe answered and to my surprise said that she would try to talk to Nick, and told us not to get our hopes up about Brey and Danny but especially Brey. After that we went to Atlanta to start the mission and hoped that we wouldn't get caught. We started as we always do first splitting up then finding a connection and finding out what all we need to break apart. A few weeks later I was one of the girlfriends of Mike Caldwell or the guy who ran all of Mr. Miller's cocaine for him.

It annoyed me to even try to have a conversation with the guy, but that thank fully ended when a bullet went through his skull when he was taking me on a date. I didn't tell the police anything and in return Mr. Miller allowed me to have dinner at his house after the funeral.

There were a lot of people there most of which I didn't know so it was easy for me to slip upstairs to look around. In one of the bedrooms I found a computer that I was happy to plug Tori into, but the second I was finished I heard a sound behind me. I turned to see Brey standing there with a pissed off expression. "I suggest you go back downstairs before I help you go down stairs" she said very menacingly.

I heard someone walking up the stairs so I said a bit louder "Well excuse me I was just trying to find a bathroom." Then a man stepped in to see the matter. He was around five eight, medium build, short brown hair, and brown eyes. "What seems to be the matter" he asked looking at Brey. She told him that she was just about to help me downstairs and he told her that was unnecessary and that he would escort there himself.

The man's name was Ethan and he was Mitch's older brother, and unlike him he was very kind and humble. He and I talked to each other for about two weeks after the funeral then we started dating. I tried really hard not to get too attached to him, but he reminded me too much of Rachel.

Their laugh, their smile, the way they both dipped their head when they say something sweet how could I not catch feelings. About a month later Mr. Miller had a party to celebrate his Daughter getting engaged, and he invited everyone who worked for him. Ethan asked me if I wanted to go with him and before thinking about how Nick and Brey's obvious presence I said yes.

Tori had finished going through the entire computer and all the other devices connect to it, and it turns out that we would not be able to destroy all of his organization at once. Since it is spread all across the globe of course all the head people would be at the party, but that leaves out everyone else that could easily operate without all of these connections. AG told us to send her a list of all the other locations and focus on making them no longer connected to each other.

This was no easy task there were going to be at least two hundred fifty people there plus extra security, so the night before Max, Aaron, and Haleigh, who had finally recovered from the last time she had a confrontation with Brey, showed up with about thirty extra tactical team members.

The night of the party Ethan told me to stay close to him and that should anything happen to go to a room in the back and wait for someone to come get me. The Miller's mansion was enormous with everything lit up with gorgeous gold accents everywhere I looked. We walked threw a marble corridor with a fountain streaming light pink water, entered the enormous ballroom. It was cream and gold with light pink flowers on each of the tables with a large area in the middle for dancing.

Ethan and I sat at a table at the edge of the dance floor with a few other couples that all seemed to know each other with me as the exception. Brey, Nick, Danny, and Chloe all sat together with their Trainer Chase and some woman who I assumed was there with him. About an hour after we had Dinner I texted Haleigh that it was time. Then I saw Chase hand the woman he was with a set of keys and She left with Chloe.

The time was exactly ten-thirty-nine when the tactical team burst through the doors and windows. It was like they were everywhere. Everyone seemed to scramble most getting shot. I ducked under the table peaking from under it to see if I could find Ethan and try to save him, but that didn't happen and I found him lying on the floor with blood seeping from his chest, eyes staring directly at me.

He gave me that last smile then took his last breath. Why can't I ever be happy I thought I have been surrounded by other people who are madly in love, and I'm the one all alone. The guy who has to focus on not lying is married, the guy whose first instinct is to kill everyone that get in his way is engaged, Haleigh has a string of people in love with her, god knows what's going on with Brey and Danny, yet I can't find a guy or girl who I love without me having to leave them or them dying.

Thinking of this I took the nearest gun and shot everyone shooting at me that wasn't dressed in tactical gear. Brey, Nick, Danny, and Chase were just sitting at their table like there was nothing was happening around them. They just sitting there drinking water as if they expected this to happen, they were surrounded by carnage and blood and seemed to almost enjoy it. This was crazy and sick going towards sadistic. I mean I always knew they were crazy and very comfortable with death, but they were able to just ignore it.

After, everyone around us either dead, or had been arrested by the tactical team, Haleigh, Hunter, Max, Aaron, and I surrounded the table where the three assassins and the whatever Danny is. Haleigh pulled her gun first and the rest of us followed as if this was going to even the odds. "What now "Chase asked taking a sip from his glass. "you all are going to jail, with everyone else here" Haleigh said.

They looked at each other then let out a small laugh which was very unsettling. "you can't be serious" Nick said, and she told him that she was. By that time the fourteen tactical team guys were surrounding them as well. "Well that's going to happen right" Danny chimed in, while the tactical team moved in closer. "Hunter, you should leave, I really like Tori and I'm not looking forward to sending you to her in a box" Brey said. "Who would have thought that you would be leading this whole thing, and thank you so much for helping me win this bet" Brey said to Haleigh while Nick and Danny just rolled their eyes. Then Max and Aaron stepped closer and Nick told them that is was a bad idea, but they and the tactical team didn't feel the need to listen.

The second Aaron grabbed Brey he pretty much sealed the fate of the entire Tactical team. He grabbed her arm and she snatched his hand then slammed his head into the table. The she stood driving her knee into his stomach a few times forcing him to spit up blood, and finally knocked him out with a punch in the face.

Next, she took his gun and shot the four guys behind her. While that was happening, across the table the four guys behind Nick tried to rush him, and were met with a concussion and a bullet to the head. Beside him Chase had killed the two men that tried to grab him by stabbing them in the throat with a butter knife. While the other two were fortunate enough to get their neck snapped and windpipe crushed. Across the table the last two team members grabbed Danny and pulled him to the ground, and he stabbed then with something that was in his hand. Their mouths started to foam and they started to shake, then they fell to the ground.

The four of us formed a semi-circle around Brey, Nick, and Danny. Haleigh and Hunter put their guns down, but Max and I kept ours trained on Chase and Danny. Then Hunter punched Nick and Haleigh lunged directly at Brey. The Two boys squared off and Nick said that he was sorry for what was about to happen then they started to fight.

Where Haleigh just ran straight for Brey and tried to kick her in the head. Brey blocked it, grabbed her leg, and flipped her knocking the wind out of her. Then she walked over to her, pulled her up off the ground and knocked her out cold with a punch to the face. Meanwhile Nick and hunter were exchanging blows until Nick kicked him in the center of his chest and proceeded to choke him till he lost consciousness.

Max tried to charge her, but she took his gun, pistol whipped him, and while she was distracted I did what I though Haleigh would want me to I shot Brey in the stomach. The only problem was that the entire upper half of the dress was bullet proof. That ladies and gentlemen is when I realized that I was going to die, not when Chase aimed his gun for my head, not when Brey threw a knife at me, not when Danny shoved something in my side, and not when Nick aimed his gun for my chest.

I don't know which one of those actually killed me but that is how I died. I felt the blood leaving my body and everything just dropped twenty degrees in seconds then I stepped out of my body and watched the world around me continue to play. They grabbed Hunter, Max, Aaron, and Haleigh and put them in one of the cars outside and put me in a body bag in the trunk. Then Danny blew up the mansion, and he drove the car about three miles away. The three of them said a few words over my body and I heard Brey say "I'm sorry Emily". That was the first time that I heard her ever say sorry and not in a sarcastic way.

After that was all done Brey was the one who closed my eyes for me, and that's when I saw them. They were standing over on the other side of the road I walked over to these two dressed all in white and they asked if I was ready. I took Rachel's and Ethan's hands and started walking towards the end of the road that seemed a lot lighter than where I was standing. They Both gave me their award-winning smiles, and with the only two people that I have ever really loved I walked into my afterlife.

Milton Keynes UK
Ingram Content Group UK Ltd.
UKHW020825141124
451205UK00012B/735

9 781869 811174